THE ZOMBIE CHASERS

ZOMBIES OF THE CARIBBEAN

BY JOHN KLOEPFER

ILLUSTRATED BY
DAVID DEGRAND

HARPER
An Imprint of HarperCollinsPublishers

Library of Congress Cataloging-in-Publication Data
Kloepfer, John.
  Zombies of the Caribbean / by John Kloepfer ; illustrated by
David DeGrand. — First edition.
    pages cm. — (The zombie chasers ; 6)
  ISBN 978-0-06-229024-3
  Summary: "The zombie chasers head to the high seas in
search of a cure for the rezombified nation"— Provided by
publisher.
    [1. Zombies—Fiction. 2. Pirates—Fiction. 3. Cruise ships—
Fiction. 4. Caribbean Area—Fiction.] I. DeGrand, David,
illustrator. II. Title.
PZ7.K6845Zr 2014   2014022033
[Fic]—dc23   CIP
                                                           AC

    14 15 16 17 18   CG/RRDH   10 9 8 7 6 5 4 3 2 1

First Edition

For Annie, Digby, and Toby

—J. K.

For Nody

—D. D.

CHAPTER

The Florida sky was pitch black and speckled with sparkling stars. The warm air hung thick with the stink of rotting flesh. It was a smell Zack Clarke had grown used to, a fact he wished wasn't true.

The whole scene was all too familiar. Zack and his friends were zooming down the highway toward the ocean to escape the undead hordes. They hoped to find Bunco's cruise ship and sail off the mainland. They needed a safe place to regroup and figure out a new antidote for the super zombie virus now spreading through Florida.

Zack's sister, Zoe, floored the gas pedal, and the engine vroomed as she wove the Jeep around zombie hitchhikers staggering across the asphalt. Her BFF, Madison, rode shotgun with her dog, Twinkles, sitting on her lap. The little Boggle pup stuck his head out the side of the moving vehicle, his ears pinned back, tongue flapping in the breeze. Zack sat scrunched in the backseat between his best friends, Rice and Ozzie, on his left and Olivia on his right.

He nudged Rice with a sharp elbow. "Dude," he said. "Quit hogging the seat."

"I'm not even," Rice said, taken aback. "Besides, you're way skinnier than me."

"That doesn't mean you get to smoosh all up on me," he said.

"Could we just get along for a few minutes, please?" Olivia asked politely. "Thanks."

Olivia Jenkins was Madison's Canadian cousin, the original Vital Veganite and the last remaining zombie antidote after Madison had inadvertently ingested a pepperoni during their school trip to New York City.

After the entire country rezombified, they had to track Olivia all the way to Bunco's Fun World, an amusement park in Orlando where she was on vacation with her family. Once they'd saved Olivia from the undead masses, they attempted to unzombify her parents, Conrad and Ginny, as well as her older brother, Ben. Unfortunately, Rice accidentally turned them into super zombies by adding Spazola Energy Cola to the antidote formula.

Not a good move.

The super zombies her family transformed into were smarter, stronger, faster, and more coordinated than any other zombie they had ever encountered. Even worse, Olivia's antidote didn't work on them. Now they needed to find a way to reverse the super zombie virus before the slime really hit the fan.

How did everything get so messed up? Zack wished they could just go back in time and do it all over again. But wishing wasn't going to solve anything. At least they hadn't been eaten by a pack of super zombie maniacs.

"Are we there yet?" Rice asked in a whiny little-kid voice.

"I swear if you ask that one more time, Rice," said Zoe, "I'm going to revoke your speaking privileges."

"You can't stop me from talking, Zoe."

"Try me," she said.

"Are we there yet?" Rice asked with a smirk.

Zoe's arm shot into the backseat, reaching for him with one hand. Rice squealed and flinched away.

"Zoe!" Zack snapped. "Focus on the road, will you?"

Zoe glared at Rice in the rearview and then calmed herself with an exasperated sigh.

"Don't let him bother you," Olivia said. "He's just trying to get under your skin."

"Ew," Zoe said. "I don't want him anywhere near my skin. Might get a nerd infection."

"Just ignore the little super-zombifying doofus," Madison said. "It's easy. I do it all the time."

Ozzie ignored the pointless back-and-forth and instead studied a map on his smartphone. "We should be there any minute."

Any minute, Zack thought. *Any minute and we'll be*

off the mainland and away from the super zombies Rice accidentally created.

Zack squinted through the windshield. He could see the coastline in the distance. A large cruise ship anchored at the marina towered over the rest of the boats in the port. Behind the cruise ship loomed a massive pirate ship.

"Whoa!" Rice exclaimed at the sight of the pirate ship. "I know what that is!"

"Well, are you going to tell us?" Madison asked. "Or are you just going to geek out privately?"

"That's the *Jolly Roger*! It's one of Bunco's Fun World rides. You actually get to go out on the high seas and live like a pirate for a day."

"Sounds cool, Rice," Zack said. "But our cruise ship awaits."

"Come on, dude, cruise ship, schmooz-ship," Rice said. "Let's take the pirate ship."

"No way," Olivia said. "If we're going to un-super-zombify my family, we're not taking some stupid pirate ship."

Zoe hit the brakes a little too hard and Zack shot forward in his seat as the Jeep jerked to a stop. It was time to ditch their ride and make a run for the cruise ship.

"Let's roll," Zoe said, throwing the gearshift into park.

"No time to play pirates, Rice. Looks like we've got some stragglers about," Ozzie warned them. His head swiveled as he assessed the nearby danger.

A horde of undead Floridians amassed in the seaport parking lot. Waves of zombified figures staggered across the pavement, blocking the dock leading out to the cruise ship.

"Where are they all coming from?" Madison asked.

Zack glanced to his left, where a long stream of elderly zombies stumbled out of a retirement community across the street. "Uh-oh," he said. "We've got some serious cheek-pinchers, eight o'clock."

The gang flung open the doors and hopped out of the Jeep. Rice and Olivia each grabbed one of the two buckets of antidote gumballs they'd managed to salvage from Bunco's factory.

As they took off through the rampaging swarm of old-timey brain-gobblers, Zack quickly doubled back for his trusty baseball bat. He raced to the Jeep and snatched it out of the trunk.

Zack ran to catch up with the rest of the gang, but an elderly zombie lady shambled toward him. The undead grandma hobbled on her walker. Her sunscorched skin was caked brown and in the process of chipping away like an old paint job. The zombie bared hideous blood-stained dentures as it snarled and gargled green bile in the back of its throat. Dodging and weaving through the undead sludge, Zack swung his bat at the thing's head, but the rezombified senior staggered out of the way. Zack whiffed hard and lost his balance. He fell to the pavement, right in the path of an old zombie codger in a wheelchair. The undead old-timer overreached for Zack and flopped to the ground next to him. Thick dark slobber like black tar ran out of its mouth. Strands of rotting flesh hung off its chin like pulled taffy.

Zack scrambled to his feet and leaped over the old geezer. *"Blargh!"* Before Zack could make his escape, the zombie grandma lunged in front of him. He was trapped.

BLAOW! Ozzie came out of nowhere and delivered an aerial roundhouse kick to the zombie woman's temple. *"Phlarckgh!"* The zombie grandma spun around, spewing dark flecks of infectious matter into the air like an automatic sprinkler. The zombie then let out a defeated groan and dropped to the cement. *"Blarghklph!"* The growing mass of sunburned zombies groaned and yacked up bodily fluids as they closed in on Zack and Ozzie.

Zack dodged the swiping arms of an undead beach bum wearing nothing but a tank top and a Speedo.

"Run!" Ozzie shouted.

"Hurry!" Olivia yelled, pointing toward Bunco's cruise ship, the *Fun World*. "This way!"

Hustling through the thickening throng of brain-craving mutants, Zack and Ozzie caught up to Zoe, Rice, and Madison. Olivia sprinted up the platform after Twinkles, leading the pack. They quickly raised the boarding staircase and gathered safely on the *Fun World*'s main upper deck.

"Can you steer this thing out of here, Oz?" Zack asked.

"Does a zombie eat brains for breakfast?" Ozzie responded with a chuckle, and then took off to the cruise ship's control room. "I'll be back in a sec."

Not more than a minute later, the ship's horn let out two low, bellowing honks that sounded like a tuba's. At the stern of the ship the propellers started to churn slowly. The MV *Fun World* pulled away from the dock and began to point its snout out at the vast Atlantic.

Zack gazed back at the dock, wondering how long it would be until they could return. The words *maybe never* popped into his head, but he shook the thought from his brain. In the distance, a long convoy of vehicles streamed into the seaport's parking lot. Zack recognized those undead faces. Cousin Ben and his super zombie minions were hot on their trail.

"We're being followed." Zack shuddered.

"Are you kidding me?" Rice said. "They figured out how to hot-wire those cars? They must be getting smarter!"

Down below, the super zombies jumped off their vehicles and lumbered hurriedly toward the docks.

There were at least two dozen of them, maybe more. Their eyeballs glared fiercely at Zack. Cousin Ben stood at the forefront of his super zombie crew, grunting heavily and shaking his fist as the MV *Fun World* set sail just in the nick of time.

"So long, suckers!" Rice let out a loud whoop before high-fiving Zack.

Zack watched the super zombie horde get smaller as the megaship cruised out onto the ocean. The sun rose over the horizon. He breathed a sigh of relief that at least for the time being they were safe from any undead peril.

"Come on, Zack," Rice said. "Let's get a little R and R, man."

"Okay." Zack nodded. "Wait, where'd the girls go?" He looked around the empty deck as Rice shrugged his shoulders. A few moments later, Olivia, Madison, and Zoe emerged from one of the ship's sundeck stations.

Madison held a portable satellite radio in one arm and her little pup, Twinkles, in the other. As Olivia and Zoe set up the deck chairs, Madison fiddled with the radio, flipping through the channels.

"Ugh," Madison groaned, trying to find some music on the radio. "This thing has, like, zero reception." As she turned the dial, Zack could hear nothing but static. Then a voice came over the airwaves.

"Wait," Rice stopped her. "Go back."

She rolled her eyes and turned the radio back to the voice. It was a newscaster for a Canadian broadcast.

"It has been confirmed. America has rezombified. Anyone affected by the BurgerDog virus from the outbreak six months ago has mysteriously transformed back into a brain-craving lunatic. . . ."

Tell me something we don't know, Zack thought.

"This just in: the newest outbreak is not confined to American soil. Zombie attacks are popping up all over the globe. London, Paris, Madrid, Moscow, Tokyo, Hong Kong. Every major city around the world is under attack!"

Okay, Zack thought. *I guess we didn't know that.*

CHAPTER 2

ack's mouth gaped at the radio. "Did you guys just hear that?" he said as Ozzie returned from the ship's control room.

"What's going on?" Ozzie said. He shot them all a funny look.

"Looks like we've got a worldwide zombie epidemic on our hands, bro!" said Rice.

Ozzie's eyes bugged out of their sockets. "That is not cool," he said. "Do they know why?"

"They didn't say, but it was probably tourists," Zack surmised. "You know, unzombified people who traveled outside the country after the first outbreak."

"Nobody had any idea they were going to rezombify," Madison said. "It must have all started with them."

"What're we gonna do?" Ozzie said, scratching his chin, deep in thought.

"I think we should definitely stop the super zombies before we worry about unzombifying everyone else," Olivia said.

"Yeah," said Zoe. "If we don't figure out an antidote for these super zombie freaks, we're all totally doomed!"

"That's why we need to find the jellyfish," Rice said.

"Will you stop talking about jellyfish, nerdbrain?" Zoe said. "Let us please all remember what happened the last time we listened to old Ricey-poo."

"We're going to need a zombie expert for this," Madison said.

"Ahem," Rice cleared his throat and gestured to himself. "Right here."

"Not you, sludge-for-brains," Zoe said. "A real expert."

"I am a real expert," Rice said.

"You call creating an entire new race of super zombies being an expert?" Olivia scoffed.

"I mean, kind of," said Rice. "Who else can really say that?"

"All in favor of never listening to what Rice has to say ever again say aye," Zoe said.

"Aye aye," Madison said.

"Chill out, guys," Zack chimed in. "It wasn't Rice's fault. He was just trying to help."

"Thanks, bro," Rice said, sounding a little hurt. "I knew you'd have my back."

"Well," Zack said, "I hate to say it, buddy, but you might actually be a little out of your depth here."

Rice scoffed at his BFF.

"I mean, maybe we should try to find someone else out there with more expertise before it's too late," Zack explained.

A long pause followed.

"Fine," said Rice, pouting a tad that his friends no longer considered him zombie expert extraordinaire. "Supposedly there's this one guy who might be able to help us out."

"Who is it, dorkbrain?" Zoe said. "Spit it out."

"His name is Nigel Black," Rice told them. "Duplessis was friends with him in college. He used to have his own TV show where he explored uninhabited regions searching for the most rare and bizarre creatures in the world. He became obsessed with zombies after he discovered signs of an ancient zombie attack during an archaeological expedition in China. And rumor has it he once encountered the undead while excavating an Egyptian tomb. But there wasn't any substantial proof, and everyone thought he was crazy. He dropped off the grid after that. No one's seen him in years."

"Okay," said Madison. "So how are we supposed to find this guy?"

Zoe whipped out the smartphone from her back pocket. "Gimme a sec. I'll see if we can pull him up." A few seconds later, her eyebrows angled down into a scowl. "All it says is stuff about his dumb TV show."

nigel black

web videos news images shopping

nigel.jpg

"Aw, man!" Rice said. "This guy could be anywhere—"

"Wait!"

"Wait what?"

"The Wikipedia entry says he retired to Nassau."

"That's awesome," Ozzie said. "Nassau's not that far from here."

"Come on, guys, seriously?" Rice said. "Wikipedia is not exactly a solid lead. Are we really going on some wild-goose chase to find this guy? I mean, how do we know he's even still alive?"

"I'll admit it's a long shot," Zack said. "But he may be our only hope."

"Yeah, we have to give it a try," said Olivia. "Unless someone has a better plan."

Rice raised his hand.

"Except for you." Olivia glared at him. "Last time you had a brilliant plan you super-zombified my whole family."

Rice put his hand down slowly and stuck out his bottom lip.

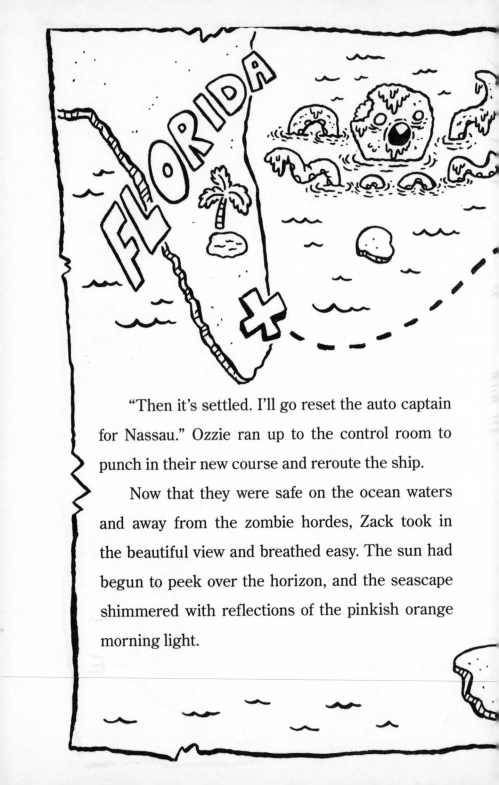

"Then it's settled. I'll go reset the auto captain for Nassau." Ozzie ran up to the control room to punch in their new course and reroute the ship.

Now that they were safe on the ocean waters and away from the zombie hordes, Zack took in the beautiful view and breathed easy. The sun had begun to peek over the horizon, and the seascape shimmered with reflections of the pinkish orange morning light.

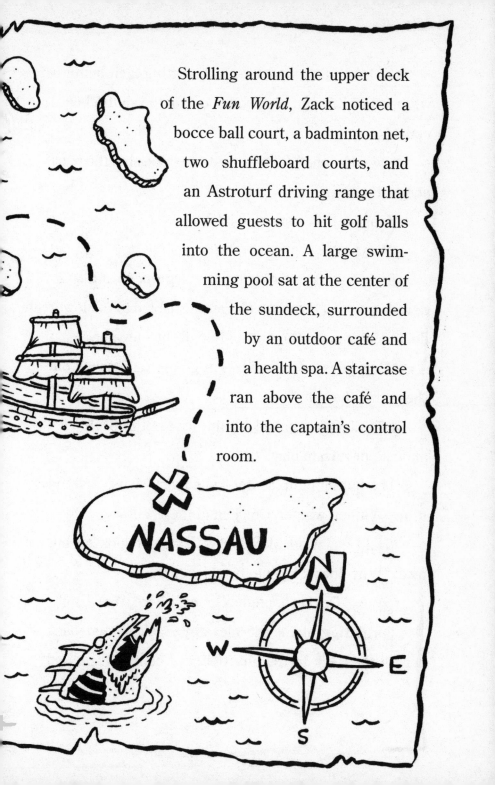

Strolling around the upper deck of the *Fun World*, Zack noticed a bocce ball court, a badminton net, two shuffleboard courts, and an Astroturf driving range that allowed guests to hit golf balls into the ocean. A large swimming pool sat at the center of the sundeck, surrounded by an outdoor café and a health spa. A staircase ran above the café and into the captain's control room.

NASSAU

N

W

E

S

Ozzie and Rice were currently getting their behinds whipped by Zoe and Madison at one of the shuffleboard courts.

"Over the line!" Rice protested as Zoe shot the puck across the board.

"Was not!" Zoe shouted back.

"Was too!"

Zack walked away from the argument and wandered by one of the glass elevators that led to the lower deck. He pressed the button to call the elevator.

"Hey, guys," Zack said. "I'm going to go check out the rest of the ship."

"Wait!" Olivia called to him across the deck. "It's almost our turn to play!"

The button lit up as Zoe yelled victoriously behind him, "Winner, winner. Chicken dinner!"

"Hold on," said Madison with a sour look on her face. "Why does it have to be chicken?"

"Zack!" Olivia shouted. "Get over here. We're up!"

Forgetting about the elevator, Zack jogged back across the deck to the shuffleboard court. Ozzie and

Rice were sulking off to the side after losing to the girls.

Zack shot the puck across the waxed cement surface. Before the puck reached the other side of the board, there came a loud and punctuated thump from across the deck. They all turned, looking with confusion in the direction of the noise.

"Could just be one of the turbines clunking," Ozzie wagered a guess.

The kids went quiet and listened. Twinkles growled in the sea-swept silence.

They could hear waves lapping at the sides of the ship and the hum of the motor from the engine room belowdecks.

Zack squinted through the Caribbean sunshine. There was no other ship on the water, and they were the only ones on board. Twinkles continued to growl, baring his little canine teeth.

"It's okay, Twinkles," Zack said. "We're safe."

"Come on, it's nothing. Let's keep playing," said Madison.

Olivia took her turn now, pushing the puck with the shuffleboard stick.

THUMP! THUMP! THWACK! Something was pounding savagely behind the elevator doors.

"Okay," Zack said, pausing the shuffleboard game once again. "That was no engine."

DING! The elevator doors parted and a raucous crew of zombified cruise staff busted onto the upper

deck. There were lifeguards in green swim trunks and rezombified waiters in formal dinner wear. A cabin steward in a pastel-colored Caribbean shirt and white shorts dragged its feet across the deck. It stared at them with a dead-eyed sneer. Its mouth hung open and thick blobs of drool dribbled down its chin.

Twinkles charged toward the growing throng of ravenous brain-craving cruise ship employees. "Arf! Arf!"

The undead cruise staff staggered along the sides of the pool. They cornered Zack and the gang against the bow of the ship. There was no place to run. Nowhere to hide.

They had no other option but to throw down and fight.

In a flash, Zack grabbed a spare shuffleboard stick. "You want some?" he shouted at the rezombified crew.

"Come and get it!" He gripped the shuffleboard stick like a bo staff and struck a ninja pose.

"Hold them off!" Ozzie said. "I'll be back in a second." As Zack and the others squared off against the undead, Ozzie bounded through the zombie fray and up the steps to the Astroturf driving range. A few moments later, Ozzie sprinted back down, brandishing four shiny titanium golf clubs that glinted in the sunlight. He tossed one each to Rice, Madison, and Olivia, keeping the fourth for himself.

Rice swung one of the golf clubs and conked the rezombified cabin steward in the noggin with a bone-cracking *thwap*. The brain-gobbling flesh-eater flipped over the rail and landed with a splat into a lifeboat. "One down, a bunch more to go. . . ."

"Unzombify them, Rice!" Zoe shouted.

Rice raced over to their supply of antidote gumballs sitting by the base of the stairs to the control room. He picked up both buckets and turned to face the undead throng of cruise ship staffers.

"Rice, watch out!" Ozzie shouted from across the

deck as a rogue zombie waiter staggered around the corner. Rice spun on his heel, but the zombie toppled right into him. They crashed to the ground, and both buckets of gumballs flew out of Rice's grip.

Zack's jaw dropped as their antidote gumball supply cascaded onto the deck and rolled over the side of the ship.

"No!" Rice screamed. He dove headfirst like a baseball player sliding into second base. He hugged the floor and scooped up as many gumballs as he could before the rest of the orange-and-blue antidote spilled into the ocean.

Zoe bounded across the deck and snagged a badminton racket out of a bin. She spun like a kung fu

ballerina and *thwapped* one of the oncoming zombies across the face. The racket strings stung its cheek with little red squares.

"*Blargh!*"

Olivia sprinted over to help her as the zombie came back for seconds. *POW!* Olivia kicked her leg straight out and nailed the undead freak square on its rump.

As the kill-crazy cruise ship staff stumbled along the deck, Ozzie unleashed a relentless barrage of karate chops.

"*Phlarghf!*"

WHAP!

BAM!

"*Sphglurghplf!*"

"*Zchwquelgph!*"

BOP! Ozzie froze in place, flexing his nunchaku after the last blow.

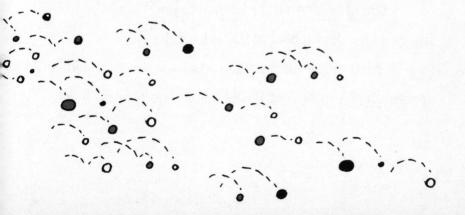

A trio of subhuman lunatics careened over the railing and into the lifeboat at the side of the ship.

"I don't think so, bucko!" Madison sidestepped a rezombified waiter and bashed it in the face with her golf club, wiping out the sunburned maniac.

"*Blarghph!*" The zombie flipped over the side rail and fell thirty-plus feet, landing in the ocean with a plunk.

One by one they took out the rest of the zombies. Madison and Olivia began to lift the conked-out bodies and toss them into the lifeboat.

"Hey, guys," Rice said, returning with his supply of salvaged gumballs. "I saved some."

"Good work, Rice," Zack said, clapping the zombie slime off his hands.

"Yeah," said Zoe. "Good work being a big old klutz."

"Hey!" said Rice. "I skinned my knee trying to save these gumballs, so I'd appreciate a little compassion."

"Maybe Twinkles will kiss it and make it better," Madison said as she and Olivia lowered the crank on the lifeboat of undeath.

"Now that we've zombie-proofed the ship, can we please hit the road or the water or whatever?" said Zoe. "We've gotta find Nigel Black. This whole zombie apocalypse thing is really starting to cramp my style."

Zack watched the zombie horde float away for good

as they continued on their way to Nassau. *Good riddance,* he thought. But he knew it wasn't over yet. He crossed his fingers on both hands and the big toes on each of his feet. They were going to need all the luck they could get.

CHAPTER

The midday sun blazed down on the tanning deck as the megaship cruised into Nassau. Zoe lay back in her pool chair next to Olivia and Madison, relaxing, catching some rays. They were all sporting sunglasses and sipping juice cocktails with little umbrellas in them.

Zack turned his focus to Nassau and the approaching coastline. The beach was strangely uninhabited, but the remnants of spring-breaking sunbathers were scattered everywhere. All kinds of chairs and umbrellas were left unattended.

Smartphones and iPads, books and magazines were strewn on the beach, along with Frisbees and a flattened volleyball net.

Once Ozzie docked the cruise ship, they hurried down the plank to the seashore. Jumping onto the beach, Zack's feet sank into the white tropical sand. It felt good to be on land again.

"Look at all this stuff!" Olivia said, plucking a transistor radio and a few iPhones out of the sand.

Madison picked a copy of *USA Weekly* off the beach and shook the sand out of the pages of the tabloid. "OMG!" she said. "What's-her-face is dating what's-his-face again!"

"Wait," Zoe said. "I thought they were, like, totally done with each other?"

"That's fantastic," Zack said, rolling his eyes a little. "Now let's go."

"First of all, little bro," Zoe sneered at Zack. "You don't tell us what to do."

"Yeah, I do," Zack said. "When my older sister's acting like a seven-year-old."

"Umm, I'm pretty sure you don't," she said, and crossed her arms, shooting him an irritated glare.

"Zack, seriously, though," Olivia said. "Where are we even going to start looking for this guy?"

"Yeah," said Madison. "Are we just going to search this entire island?"

"If that's what it takes," he said. "I don't know what else to do."

"We're open to suggestions," Ozzie said. "If anyone has a better idea . . ."

Olivia rubbed her chin while they all thought. A few seconds later, her eyes lit up. "This Nigel Black dude used to catch wildlife for a living, right? And now he's retired. So unless he sits around all day doing nothing, wouldn't he do what he loves most? I'm guessing Nigel Black is still some kind of fisherman." She pulled a tourist map of the island out of the sand and wiped some zombie slime off it. "Here," she said, showing them the map. "There are two bait and tackle shops on opposite sides of the island. Why don't we start there?"

"Good idea, Olivia," Zoe said. "Boys versus girls.

Whoever finds Nigel Black first wins."

"What do we win?" Rice asked.

"You don't win anything," she said. "Because you're you."

"Arf!" Twinkles chirped, ready to follow Zack, Rice, and Ozzie inland.

"Except for you, Twinklie-poo," Madison said, picking up her pup and kissing him on the head. "You're coming with the girls."

Twinkles flashed a pair of weary puppy dog eyes at the boys and whimpered lamely as Madison carried her pet off with Zoe and Olivia.

"We ready to do this?" Rice asked.

"You know it," Zack said, giving his boy a fist bump.

"Let's roll out," Ozzie hollered, and trotted inland toward the center of the island in search of Nigel Black.

Each holding a golf club and a couple of antidote gumballs in his pocket, the three boys snuck under a sign that read: WELCOME TO NASSAU. Ahead of them a massive swarm of rezombified spring breakers coursed through the streets.

Shirtless college boys wobbled in the daylight, their bodies sunbaked with peeling skin. Zombie girls wearing short denim shorts and bikini tops went wild, snarling and clawing. Flesh fell off the rezombified spring breakers' sun-scorched shanks like meat off braised short ribs. A pig roast aroma wafted through the thick, sticky Bahamian air, which made Zack oddly hungry. The Nassau horde was a walking-dead barbecue.

The sun highlighted the satanic grimaces fixed on the zombies' faces. At close range, the undead eyes were crazed with psychotic rage, bloodshot, and oozing blobs of lemon yellow slime.

The boys dodged and weaved through the zombie mayhem, knocking out undead beach bums left and right with their drivers and nine irons.

"Look," Zack cried, pointing toward a wooden sign hanging over a storefront that read: BAIT AND TACKLE. "Up there!"

"Zack, watch out!" Rice shouted as two zombie spring breakers lumbered up behind him.

Zack spun around and ducked as a shirtless undead beefcake swiped for his head. He could hear a gravelly crunch in the zombie freak's shoulder as its arm whizzed past his face. Zack leaped back and bumped into another zombie coming from the other direction. A twentysomething girl in a bikini raked her claws back and forth, clutching at the air. The bikini-clad zombie girl's eyeball hung from its socket and dangled to her cheekbone from behind a pair of cracked sunglasses.

"Get out of there, bro!" Ozzie called to his friend.

Zack almost got caught in the melee of undead flesh-eaters, but he managed to muscle his way out of the zombie scrum.

The three boys weaved through the island of mutant spring breakers and rushed inside the bait shop. Zack locked the doors behind them and turned to have a look around the store. A thick, pungent odor hit his nostrils. He choked, covering his mouth with his shirt collar. Everything was turned completely upside down. Buckets of chum and sardines spilled across the floor. Fishing poles, nets, and rotating racks of bait hooks were knocked over, booby-trapping the ground.

Zack, Ozzie, and Rice split up to explore the shop, treading through the ankle-deep live bait.

Framed photographs hung on the wall. All of them featured a tan, bald-headed man with a thick, bushy beard posing with strange creatures in different parts of the world.

"Hey, guys," said Zack. "I think we're in the right place."

"Is that him?" Ozzie asked.

"Think so," Rice said, pulling out his smartphone. "Lemme check."

While Rice inspected the photographs against the Google images, a loud crash rang out from the back of the shop. Zack's heart skipped a beat.

"What was that?" he asked in a whisper. They listened but heard only the muffled drone of the zombies outside.

"Come on," Ozzie said. "Let's go check the back."

Quickly, the boys trudged down the short hallway and opened the door to the back room. Except for a sharp beam of sunlight slicing through the only window, the room was too dark to see into from the doorway. Zack flicked the light switch, but the power was out.

"Nigel?" Zack asked softly as they stepped nervously into the shadowy room.

"Blarrggghh!" a zombie howled, and lunged out of the darkness.

"Whoa!" Ozzie jumped back into the hallway.

Out stumbled a scraggly zombie around sixty years old. Its tattered fisherman's outfit hung from its lanky frame. Its skin was wrinkled like a raisin, and it smelled like boiled cafeteria meat.

"I don't think that's Nigel," Rice said.

"Me neither," Zack said.

Ozzie put up his hands, preparing to grapple the undead fisherman.

Its decrepit hand was wrapped around a fishing pole. The zombie cast its

line at Ozzie, who dodged the airborne hook. The fishing hook flew through the stinking heat and snagged Zack by the shirt collar.

"Ahhhh!" Zack cried as the rezombified fisherman pulled back on the line and reeled him in. Zack slipped on the wet floor and ran in place like he was trying to run on a carpet of gumballs.

"*Glarphle!*" The zombie lunged for Zack, and they both hit the fish-covered floor with a yucky splat. The zombie crawled on top of him, clacking its undead maw repeatedly. "*NOM-NOM-NOM!*" Strands of toxic saliva stretched and snapped as the thing smacked its decomposing lips.

Zack shoved the palm of his hand upward under the jaw of the growling zombie to keep its flesh-hungry mouth away. He gripped him by the throat with the other hand. The zombie man gargled and bit the air ferociously.

"Hold on, buddy!" Rice flipped his backpack off his shoulder and unzipped the bag, pulling out a small bottle of ginkgo biloba. He twisted the cap off the bottle and poured out a heap of ginkgo capsules. He ran over to where Zack lay on his back and slammed the handful of ginkgo into the fisherman's mouth. The zombie sputtered the capsules back into Rice's face.

"Ahhhh!" Rice shrieked, and flinched back.

"Give him more!" Zack shouted, still fighting on his back. His hands were slipping. "He's going to eat my face off!"

The zombie fisherman's mouth was six inches from Zack's nose. Zack strained his muscles with every ounce of strength he had, but the zombie had too much leverage. His arms buckled like someone trying to bench-press too much weight.

Rice reached for the zombie's hair and grabbed a fistful, pulling back hard. The undead fisherman reeled away from Zack and screeched as Rice drove the whole bottle of ginkgo into the zombie's slime-webbed maw.

"*Gluggle-glarghle!*"

The undead flesh-guzzler chowed down on the ginkgo and slumped to the floor in a full-on zombie coma.

Zack rose to his feet and grimaced. His entire backside was wet with rotting fish water. A little splash of vomit rose from his belly and burned the back of his throat.

"Ah, Zack," Rice said, and plugged his nose. "You reek, son!"

"Shake it off, Zacky boy," Ozzie said. "Come on, let's see if we can find anything that tells us where this Nigel Black dude might be."

The boys edged cautiously into the back room. Outside, the air still hummed steadily with the incessant wailing of the undead spring breakers.

Quickly, Zack, Rice, and Ozzie searched Nigel's office for any hints as to the washed-up explorer's whereabouts.

BANG! SLAM! CRASH! Glass shattered somewhere in the front of Nigel's shop.

"Looks like we're about to be the bait," said Ozzie. "If we don't want to get tackled, let's grab what we can and get out of here!" Zack snagged a stack of important-looking folders out of the file cabinet while Rice snatched a DVD box set of Nigel Black's *Unnatural Wonders*. Ozzie folded up what was on the desk: a sticky heap of yellow Post-its and a blueprint of some kind.

Rice stuffed the papers and DVDs into his back-pack. Zack lifted open the window as Ozzie barricaded the door with Nigel's desk. They all hopped onto the windowsill. The island zombies stormed through the shop, grunting and growling on the other side of the office door.

The boys hit the ground outside and hightailed it away from the bait and tackle shop. They trekked through the island shrubbery, staying off the zombified streets. Soon, they reached a sandy path leading back to the beach and the cruise ship.

The ocean tide lapped at their feet as they sprinted along the damp sand. Ozzie rounded the point to the next bay, followed by Zack and then Rice. From there

they could
see the *Fun
World* cruise
ship towering over
the beach, which was
now overrun by undead
vacationers. The girls were
fighting off an endless herd
of undead sunbathers and island dwellers as they made
their way to the ship.

But even at a distance Zack could already see the
zombies were taking over the pathway leading to the
dock.

"Hurry up, guys!" Zack shouted. "Looks like they're
in over their heads!"

The boys rushed down the seacoast as fast as they

could. When they reached the girls, Zoe, Madison, and Olivia were out of breath, losing more and more ground to the gathering horde of beach bums.

"Nice of you to show up!" Zoe blasted one of the zombies in the noggin with a beach umbrella.

"Did you find Nigel Black?" Olivia asked as she slammed an oncoming zombie hard in the jaw with her elbow.

"No, but we got some intel on him," Zack said.

"Thank goodness! We have to get out of here. There are too many of these zombified spring breakazoids!" Madison shouted, clobbering one of the bikini-clad zombie surfer chicks in the abdomen with a stiff side kick.

They turned to make a run through the throng of rezombified mutants, but the undead mob was too thick to pass through.

"We have to swim out and climb up the dock!" Ozzie pointed out to the water and they took off running through the waist-deep surf.

They shimmied up the support pole underneath the dock and climbed onto the platform. The zombie herd continued to stagger up the dock toward the gangplank to the cruise ship.

"Run for it!" Zack cried, and they all sprinted back to safety before the undead spring breakers could cut them off.

CHAPTER

Once they'd placed the *Fun World* cruise ship on autopilot, Zack walked down to the middle deck and went down the narrow corridor. He pushed through the door where his friends had gathered in the luxury cabin suite to study up on Nigel Black. The place looked like an upscale hotel room. Madison, Zoe, and Olivia had already made themselves comfortable on the couch. A big-screen television and a state-of-the-art entertainment system stretched across the wall in front of them.

Zack sat down at the desk next to Ozzie and added to Ozzie's pile the files he'd grabbed from the bait shop.

"Time to get to work," Ozzie said. "The first step to

tracking down a person of interest is to gather as much intelligence as you can on them."

"What are we waiting for, Ricey-poo?" Zoe said. "Let's watch and see what we can find out."

"Yeah, yeah, hold your horses already." Rice knelt in front of the television and popped in the first DVD of Nigel Black's *Unnatural Wonders*.

"He doesn't kill these things, does he?" Madison asked, looking at the DVD packaging. "Because if all he does is catch these poor weird-looking creatures and kill them, then I don't want to watch."

"Yeah," said Olivia. "I second that emotion."

"Would you ladies take a chill pill?" Rice said. "He

doesn't kill them. He just captures them and studies them."

"OK, well, in that case . . . ," Olivia approved.

Rice walked over to the cabin window and pulled down the shade, darkening the room as the TV glowed with the show's introduction.

"Greetings," a voice said over a blank screen. "My name is Nigel Black. Welcome to *Unnatural Wonders*." The television flashed to a shot of the bow of a sailing ship. Nigel Black stepped into the frame, great gusts of oceanic wind ruffling his clothing. "Today we are on the Pacific Ocean looking for the albino electric eel said to inhabit these waters. . . ."

Rice paused the DVD. "I don't know, maybe we should go back to Nassau," he said. "This dude could still be a zombie."

"Well, if the zombie expert got himself zombified," Madison said, "he's probably not that much of a zombie expert. Just saying."

"You guys got anything over there?" Olivia asked Zack.

"Not much," Zack said. "Just some bills and some orders for fish. Nothing about where he might be. What about you, Oz?"

"No," he said. "Just a bunch of random legal documents."

"Wait a second," Zack said, looking back at Nigel's papers spread out across the tabletop. He pulled the blueprint out of the mess of papers and held it up. "Check this out."

"What is it?" Ozzie asked, looking over Zack's shoulder.

"It's a blueprint of a house," Zack said.

"That's no house," Ozzie said. "That's a freakin' fortress!"

The rest of the gang gathered around Zack and stared at the blueprint. After a long pause, Olivia pointed at the bottom left-hand corner of the plan. "I think those are coordinates."

"Good eye, cuz," Madison said. Rice punched the coordinates into his smartphone. His eyes bulged at the touch screen. He turned the phone so the rest of them

could see. Zack squinted at the search results and saw
that the coordinates matched up to a small Bahamian
island a few miles off the coast of Nassau.

"Jackpot," he said.

"Come on, girls," Rice said. "Our work here is done.
Let's go catch some rays before the sun runs out." Zoe,
Madison, and Olivia went out to the sundeck with Rice.

Zack took a deep breath and let out a long belea-
guered sigh. His eyes started to lose focus. He realized
he hadn't slept a wink in nearly twenty-four hours. He

felt Ozzie's hand clamp down on his shoulder.

"Don't worry," Ozzie said. "We're going to find this guy."

"I hope so," Zack said in a quiet voice. "I really hope so."

"Take it easy, man. I'm gonna go reroute the ship," Ozzie said, and burst out of the cabin suite in a flash.

Zack stood up from the table and lay down on the couch. He felt like taking a nap, but before he could catch a wink, a shrill bark from Twinkles chirped through the sea breeze. Half a dozen footsteps clattered down the hallway and stopped outside the door.

"Zack, come quick," Madison said, out of breath. "We've got trouble."

"What kind of trouble?" he asked, sitting up.

"Super zombie trouble," Olivia said.

"Ha-ha, nice try," said Zack. "But I'm not falling for that."

"Fifty bucks says there are super zombies chasing us right this second," Zoe exclaimed.

"Deal, easiest money I ever made." Zack shook his sister's hand.

"We're serious, Zack," Madison said. "They're on Bunco's pirate ship!"

"And they're catching up quick," said Zoe.

"Everyone on deck! Everyone on deck!" Ozzie's voice came over the intercom loudspeaker system. Zack jumped out of his seat and raced out of the cabin.

CHAPTER 5

Zack, Rice, Madison, Olivia, and Zoe stood on the ship's highest deck, looking out over the port rail. Rice peered through a pair of binoculars. "It's them all right," he confirmed.

"Let me see that," said Zack, grabbing the binoculars away from his friend.

In the distance a large ship with a skull-and-crossbones flag sailed toward them. He could make out the pale, apelike figures of the super zombies scurrying to and fro along the deck. Cousin Ben, Olivia's super zombie brother, was commanding the vessel.

"What the—" Zack murmured, and let the

binoculars dangle around his neck.

"Told ya so, little bro," Zoe said. "You owe me fifty bucks."

Zack's heart sank at the sight of Bunco's pirate ship. "Put it on my tab," he said.

Ozzie leaned out the pilothouse window, whipped out his binoculars, and surveyed the super zombie pirate ship. "Oh, snap! That's messed up." He turned to Zack. "Looks like Cousin Ben's running the show."

"Come on, Ozzie," Zoe whined as the cruise ship

plowed its bulk at a slow clip through the high seas. "Can't this thing go any faster?"

"Not really," Ozzie told her. "This thing isn't exactly built for speed."

"What are we supposed to do?" Madison said.

"They may be faster than us," Zoe said. "But we're bigger than them."

"Everybody, quick!" Zack shouted. "Grab everything you can and bring it over to this side. If they're going to try and board our ship, we're not going to make it easy on them."

As the super zombie pirate ship sailed toward their slow-moving megaship, the kids gathered up bowling balls, golf clubs, deck chairs, and anything else they could get their hands on.

Zack looked through the binoculars again and trained the lens on the front of the enemy ship. The super zombies were loading a cannon on the top deck and aiming it straight at them.

"Uh-oh!" Zack said, and turned to his friends with a shocked look on his face. "Rice, do the cannons on

Bunco's pirate ship actually work?"

"Yeah," Rice said. "Like I told you, Bunco restored the ship to its original working condition. Why?"

BOOM! The cannon cracked in the distance.

"Duck!" Zack shouted. The cannonball sailed through the air and came crashing down. The wooden deck erupted in splinters as the cannonball pierced the upper level.

BOOM! BOOM! BOOM! Three more shots rang out.

"Hit the deck!" Ozzie shouted. The kids all ducked for cover.

"What are we going to do?" Olivia shrieked.

The kids huddled together as one of the cannonballs flew through the café and spa beneath the control room. The two other shots of cannon fire drilled two jagged holes into the side of the cruise ship.

Rice peeked over the railing and yelled, "They're gonna hit us!"

Bunco's pirate ship of the undead swept up swiftly alongside the starboard flank of the *Fun World* megacruiser. The kids all braced themselves as the super-zombified clipper sideswiped their ship with a sturdy clank.

A split second later, one of the super zombies bounded off the pirate ship and grabbed on to the white-painted ladder at the hull of Bunco's cruise ship. In its hand it held one end of a rope ladder that stretched all the way across to the pirate ship. The kids watched in horror as the super zombie boarding their ship tied the rope ladder to the rungs, tethering the pirate ship to the megacruiser.

Ozzie took off like a shot back to the control room.

"Where are you going?" Zack shouted. "We need you!"

"I'll be back," he called out as he ran away. "I have to change our direction!"

"They're climbing!" Olivia yelled over the sea breeze.

"Zack!" Rice shouted. "Get ready!"

While the super zombie pirates clung to the rungs of the ladders, Zack ran to the cruise ship café and found the cannonball in a pile of rubble by the counter. He picked

up the cannonball and lugged it back to the ship's railing. He lined it up with the super zombie below and let it fall. *WHAMMO!* A direct hit sent the super zombie flailing off the ladder and splashing in the wake of the megaship's turbine propellers.

"Good aim, little bro," Zoe said. "Watch this!"

As she lifted a bocce ball over her head, the cruise ship jerked. Zoe squealed and dropped the ball away from the super zombies. "Hey! What the heck!" she yelled.

Ozzie steered away from the zombified pirate ship. The ropes tightened between the two vessels as the *Fun World* changed direction.

Some of the super zombies were flung off into the ocean while others continued to climb the ladders of the cruise ship. More and more used the taut rope lines like monkey bars and grappled their way across.

Some of them were wearing eye patches. Others wore black vests with gold trim and pirate hats. Their costumes were fitted with fancy-looking scabbards, and they were brandishing replica swords as they howled and grunted what sounded like an old sea shanty.

From the pirate ship, Cousin Ben commanded the ambush. He wore a frilly white puffy shirt and an eye patch over his right eye. Zack caught Cousin Ben's gaze and stared into his left eye. There was a flicker of intellect in the cold, blank glare looking back at him.

Cousin Ben pointed up at Olivia and bared his teeth, and then he growled. His super zombie minions peered up at Madison's Canadian cousin and locked eyes with their prey.

"Are they coming after me?" Olivia asked, her voice cracking a little.

"Don't worry, Olivia," Zack said. "We'll protect you. Right, guys?"

"Yeah!"

"Don't worry, girl," said Zoe. "We gotchoo."

"Olivia, maybe you should go to the captain's control room and stay there until the coast is clear!" Rice shouted.

"No way!" Olivia sounded angry. "I can fight zombies just as well as anyone here!"

"Olivia, please," Zack said. "You're the last antidote. We can't afford to lose you."

"We can't afford to lose this battle either," she said.

"She's right," Ozzie called down from the pilothouse. "We need all hands on deck if we're going to make it out of this!"

"Yeah, dorkbrains, let her fight," Zoe said. "She could probably take both of you with one hand tied behind her back."

"Blarghphle-gloggle!" One of the super zombies breached the ledge

and reared its ugly head over the railing.

Patches of its pale, sallow skin were beginning to turn bright pink from the beating sun. Its eyes were dark and sunken as if a day-old cadaver had just woken from a stay at the morgue.

"Hi-ya!" Madison lunged forward, wielding one of the shuffleboard shooters. She drilled the super zombie freak in its larynx with the V-shaped crux of the stick.

"*Schlarf!*" The super zombie squawked and reeled back, falling off the railing and down into the water below.

The uber undead ransackers continued to scrabble up the ladders while the kids threw all manner of debris: deck chairs, bocce balls, full cans of soda from the snack bar.

The kids picked off their undead

targets, but the super zombie pirates just kept coming, shimmying across the tightened ropes between the two vessels and climbing up the ladders of the cruise ship.

Zack stared down the hull of the ship as Ozzie continued to navigate away from the pirate ship. Both ladders running up the sides were filled with super zombies.

"You guys, we're running out of stuff to throw!" Zack shouted. "What are we gonna do?"

"Out of the way, little bro," Zoe came sprinting from the upper deck's supply room with Madison. They were each carrying an armful of bottles of suntan lotion.

Madison stopped in front of the first ladder. Zoe

stood looking down the top of the second. The two of them began to squeeze out the bottles of lotion and tanning oil, drizzling the slippery substance all over the top rungs of the ladders. The oily moisturizer dripped down from rung to rung, and the super zombies began to lose their grips and fall off, knocking one another down until there were none left.

"Yeah!" Zack shouted. "Woo-hoo!" He jumped in the air and pumped his fist.

WHOOSH! Suddenly, a fast-moving shadow passed over their heads and a loud double thump sounded on the deck. Olivia's super undead brother had landed on the cruise ship's upper deck like a swashbuckling buccaneer. They all whirled around as Cousin Ben dismounted from a length of rope tied to the mast of the pirate ship. The super zombie ringleader wrapped Olivia up with both arms.

"Get off me, Ben!" Olivia cried, trying to wriggle free from the clutches of her super-zombified older brother. "Seriously, I mean it. You're hurting me!"

"Let her go, man!" Zack yelled at the super zombie.

Cousin Ben snarled ferociously at Zack and bounded toward the railing.

"Hold it right there, el freako!" Zoe shouted. "Not another step."

Cousin Ben cackled at her as if he were amused by the threat.

"Oh, you think that's funny?" Zoe clenched her jaw and her eyes sparked with bitter fury. She gripped the handle of a badminton racket and shook it at Cousin Ben.

BOOM! The cannon exploded—only this time it wasn't a cannonball.

"Duck!" Madison shouted, and dropped to the ground.

One of the super zombies flew through the air, somersaulting and then slamming on the deck of the cruise ship with a bone-crunching crash.

The super zombie jumped to its feet and lunged toward Zoe. She swatted the undead mutant with her badminton racket. The super zombie caught the racket and ripped it out of her hand, then broke the frame clean in half.

Ozzie and Rice ran over to help Zoe with the undead super freak.

"Hey!" yelled Rice. "Pick on someone your own size!"

The super zombie growled and lunged at Rice.

"I didn't mean me!" Rice retreated from the super zombie attack and let out a high-pitched squeal.

"Let her go!" Zack continued to shout at Cousin Ben to release Olivia.

ZWOOSH! Across the way on the pirate ship, one of Cousin Ben's super zombie minions sent another rope from the mast to his undead master and commander. Cousin Ben caught the rope with one arm, holding Olivia with the other one. She squirmed, trying to elbow her older super zombie brother in the ribs, but Cousin Ben felt no pain and only tightened his grasp.

Zack sprinted full steam toward Cousin Ben, who mounted the rail, ready to make off with Olivia.

"Zack!" Olivia shouted.

Just as Cousin Ben jumped, Olivia managed to wriggle her arm free. She reached out to Zack. Zack stretched his arm out, too, and caught her firmly by the wrist. He held strong as Cousin Ben swung down. Zack had the upper hand, and Olivia, still covered in suntan lotion, slipped free from her brother's clutches.

Cousin Ben's eyes went wild with anger, and he reached back for Olivia, losing his grip on the swinging rope. The super zombie flailed and fell down to the waters below.

Zack's midsection smashed into the metal railing. His stomach bruised as Olivia thunked against the hull. She dangled over the side of the ship, clinging to Zack's hand and shrieking at the top of her lungs.

Zack felt his grasp slipping and clutched tighter.

"Zack!" she screamed, the ocean roiling below them. "Don't let go!"

Zack reached over with his other arm. He grabbed her

wrist with two hands now, which nearly flipped him over the rail and sent them both down into the super zombie–infested waters. Olivia kicked her legs, trying to get a foothold on the side of the ship, but she continued to flail.

"Help!" Zack shouted. "Someone help me! She's slipping!"

Rice raced over behind his friend. "I'm here, buddy!" He grabbed Zack around his waist. "On the count of three, we give her the old heave-ho. Hang on, Olivia!"

"One, two!" Zack shouted. "Three!" He yanked upward with all his strength and started to pull her up. She lifted her foot onto the railing and fell on top of Zack, who fell backward onto Rice. The three of them tumbled back onto the deck with a *thunk*.

"Phew," she said, brushing her hair out of her face and getting off of Zack. "Thanks, guys. That was a close one, eh?"

"Cut the ropes!" Rice shouted. "Cut the ropes!"

Zack followed his friend's gaze and looked down the side of the cruise ship where the ropes from the pirate ship were lashed to the ladders.

Ozzie was climbing deftly down one of the lotion-slick ladders with his military-issue survival knife.

PHFFT! Ozzie sliced the rope clean through, and the super zombies were flung off, dropping into the ocean deep. *PHFFT!* Ozzie clipped the second rope line before the other super zombie buccaneers could climb across. The gaggle of super zombie pirates went flying into the sea on the rope's violent whiplash.

Finally they were detached and drifting away from Bunco's pirate ship.

"Let's just make sure none of those super zombies managed to get on board," Ozzie said. "Then get the heck out of here."

"Not so fast," Zoe said. "First we have to make sure these super freaks can't catch up to us again." She pulled a flare gun out of her back pocket and aimed it at the pirate ship.

"Zoe, where'd you get that?" Zack said to his sister.

"Shhh," she said. "I found it." Zoe shot the flare directly at the top sail. The sail burst into flames and the kids all watched as the skull and crossbones disappeared in a fiery blaze. Down in the water, Cousin Ben's face twisted into a hideous grimace.

"Nice shot, Zo!" Madison high-fived her BFF while Olivia wandered back to the group studying a piece of paper in her hand.

"Hey, guys," Olivia said. Her voice sounded worried. "Take a look at this. I snagged it from Ben's pocket."

"What is it?" Zack asked.

"Let me see that." Rice swiped the paper from Olivia. "I think it's their game plan," he said. "I think I know why they want to capture her."

There was a crude drawing of a girl with the letter O next to her. The drawing showed the super zombies feeding parts of Olivia to regular zombies. The final part of the plan showed the super zombies eating the brains of the unzombified masses.

"I don't get it," Olivia said.

"They're running out of brains," Rice explained. "They need to turn regular zombies back into humans so they can feed on them. And the only way they can do that is you."

Olivia gasped in terror.

"That's disgusting!" Madison said.

"There's no way that's going to happen," Zack said. "Not on our watch. Are we ready to go, Ozzie?"

"Yep," he said. "We should be there by morning. Then hopefully we can get some answers on how to stop these super zombies before they turn everybody into brain feed."

The megacruiser roared its engines and left the super zombie pirates in its wake, stranded in the middle of the ocean. Next stop: Nigel's private fortress.

CHAPTER

A bright ray of sunlight cut through the porthole and woke Zack. He had no idea how long he had been asleep, but he felt refreshed. Sitting up in bed, he heard the engines slow down and felt the ship begin to idle in the water.

"Rise and shine, Zacky-poo," Madison called into the cabin. "We're almost there!"

Ozzie's voice came over the intercom as Zack ambled groggily on deck. "Everybody get ready to deboard. We're about to hit land." He docked the cruise ship at the small private island where they hoped to find Nigel Black.

In the blaring Caribbean sun, the six of them plus Twinkles hopped into a lifeboat one after the other. Ozzie hit the lever and lowered the boat down into the water.

As they paddled to shore, Zack could see a heavy-duty fence with barbed wire running around what looked to be the entire island. A steep, rocky slope walled off the beach, and jungle terrain grew above it.

Once on land, they climbed along the sand dune until they came to a small narrow, wooden drawbridge that crossed a moat to the electrified fence. They crossed over and stood in front of an intercom fashioned to the middle of the main gate.

Rice reached out and hit the buzzer. A few seconds later a security camera positioned just inside the fence turned and aimed its robotic gaze at the kids.

"Look!" Olivia pointed. "The camera."

"That doesn't mean anyone is here," Ozzie said. "It could be automated."

"Only one way to find out," Zack said, and began addressing the security camera as if it were an actual person. "Mr. Black, sir. My name is Zack Clarke. I'm here with some of my friends."

"We're the Zombie Chasers, dude!" Rice butted in.

"Shhhhh!" Zack made an annoyed face at Rice and raised his index finger to his pursed lips. "We came a really long way to find you. We don't know if you're in there. But if you are, please let us in. We need to speak with you. We have some new information about the zombie outbreak going on right now. . . ."

Before he could finish, the electrified fence deactivated and the main gate parted. As they entered the

private island fortress, the gates closed automatically behind them. Two rows of palm trees lined the walkway that led inland. The pathway they followed ran uphill toward a concrete facade built into the side of a hill. As they strolled through the grounds, security cameras fashioned to the treetops watched their every move.

"This is totally weird," Olivia said.

"Yeah, didn't you say he went crazy?" Madison said. "Are you sure we can trust him?"

"Yes," Rice said. "Duplessis vouched for him."

"Oh, you mean the guy who invented BurgerDog and turned everyone into zombies?" Zoe said. "That's who we're trusting these days?"

"Come on, Zoe." Rice raised an eyebrow. "He's a good guy. Everyone makes mistakes."

"Shh!" Zack said. "He might still be able to hear us."

"Hello?" Ozzie called out. "Mr. Black?"

When they stopped before the entrance to the bunker, a man's voice sounded from a speaker overhead. "Who are you? Have any of you been bitten by the zombies?"

The kids looked around at one another. "Not recently," Rice said.

"Did any zombies follow you here?" the voice asked.

"Which ones?" Rice asked. "Regular or super?"

"What do you mean?" The voice said with a hint of nervousness in his tone. "Since when is there more than one kind of zombie?"

"Well, there's the kind of zombie that walks around and tries to eat your brains," Zoe told him. "But now there's the kind that chases you down and tries to kidnap antidote people."

"We're calling them super zombies," Ozzie said.

"Sir, if you just let us in, we'll explain everything," Zack pleaded. "The super zombies didn't follow us here. And none of us can get zombified anymore."

"Unless Olivia eats a steak or something and then gets bitten by a zombie," Madison whispered.

"Could you not bring that up right now?" Olivia said. "Not really something I want to think about, cuz."

The door opened on its own, and the kids walked in cautiously. The floors, walls, and ceiling of Nigel's bunker were made of solid concrete. Rows of potted plants lined the twin hallways that split off on either side of the foyer and seemed to go on forever.

Standing across from them on the far side of the entrance hall, a figure was waiting, still as a statue. The man was well over six feet tall and wearing a protective suit made of high-grade plastic that covered his entire body. It looked like a space suit or the kind of gear government agents wear when dealing with biohazardous materials.

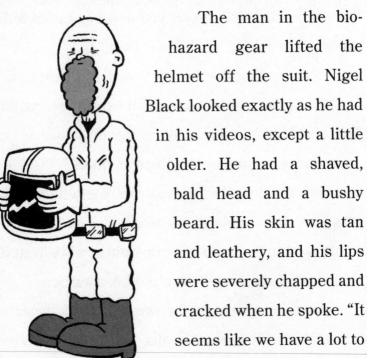

The man in the bio-hazard gear lifted the helmet off the suit. Nigel Black looked exactly as he had in his videos, except a little older. He had a shaved, bald head and a bushy beard. His skin was tan and leathery, and his lips were severely chapped and cracked when he spoke. "It seems like we have a lot to talk about," he said. "Follow me. I'll show you around while you give me some more details."

"What the heck is this place?" Zack asked as they trailed behind him down the concrete corridor.

"This bunker we're in right now is the safest place in the world," Nigel said. "Completely zombie-proof. I bought this island and began construction after Duplessis finished his BurgerDog recipe. I warned him of the dangers in using the immortal jellyfish, but he wouldn't listen. I was convinced that a zombie epidemic was only a matter of time. And I was right."

"You must know a lot about zombies," Rice piped up. "From your encounters with the undead during your expeditions. . . ."

"Ah, so you've seen my show." Nigel's brow furrowed as he blinked involuntarily and looked away. "But if you don't mind, I don't like to talk about the past. Tell me what's going on out there. Start from the beginning."

"Okay," Zack began. "So you know that almost everyone who got unzombified six months ago all mysteriously rezombified like four or five days ago. We were trapped in New York City and just barely escaped."

"Oh, my goodness," Nigel said. "That's awful. I actually had a feeling something like this would happen."

"Yeah," Rice added. "I was a zombie for a while, too, because Madison mistakenly lost her vegan antidote powers to a piece of pepperoni pizza. But then I ate the Band-Aid in Central Park and unzombified. Man, being a zombie was cool."

Nigel gave Rice a sidelong glance then looked at Madison. "But you were the antidote. . . ."

"Not anymore, mister," she said.

"That's when we tracked down Olivia, Madison's cousin," Zack said.

"That's me." Olivia raised her hand and gave an awkward smile. "Now I'm the antidote. Whoopee!" She cheered without enthusiasm.

"So we have an alternate antidote," Nigel said. "That's great!"

"Yeah, it was great." Olivia looked pointedly at Rice. "Until someone turned my brother, Ben, and my mom and dad into super zombies."

87

"How did that happen?" Nigel asked.

"I was only trying to make the new antidote even stronger," Rice jumped in, defending himself. "So I infused it with some of Bunco's Spazola Energy Cola. But it turns out that stuff has Caribbean sea plankton in the ingredients, so instead of making the antidote stronger, it actually made the zombie virus stronger, because of the—"

"Because of the jellyfish." Nigel finished Rice's sentence. "This is bad. The virus has mutated."

"You have no clue, mister," said Zoe. "Super zombies ain't no joke."

"Yeah, Nigel," Madison said. "They're way smarter and more organized."

"And your family members were the only ones?" Nigel asked.

"Well," Zack stammered, "they were . . ."

"But then when we were at the bubble gum factory something kind of not that cool happened," Rice continued.

"Okay," said Nigel as a befuddled scowl crossed his face. "Now I'm confused."

"Long story short," Ozzie said. "More zombies got exposed to the Spazola, and now the whole state of Florida is filling up with a super zombie army."

Nigel took a deep breath and sighed with a long, low grumble. "I see. Then we must act quickly. Time is of the essence."

There followed a long pause before Rice broke the silence.

"I don't see what the big deal is, you guys," he said. "All we have to do is find the jellyfish and boom: super zombie antidote."

Nigel nodded, scratching his bearded chin. "The Turritopsis nutricula would be valuable samples to have, but I don't think it will be enough to counteract the super zombie virus. We need something that will break down the jellyfish DNA already present in the viral strain."

"See?" Zoe said. "I told you we needed a real zombie expert."

Rice glared angrily in her direction. "All right, then," he said, turning back to Nigel. "What do you propose, Mr. Zombie Expert?"

"I'm quite familiar with the jellyfish breed in question," Nigel said. "And there's only one species of deep-sea dweller known to feed on them exclusively: a rare breed of giant frilled tiger shark. Its digestive system has a particular acid composition that dissolves the jellyfish's DNA. If we can get a giant frilled tiger shark, it'll be our best bet to make an antidote for these so-called super zombies."

"Then let's do it," Zack said. "Let's find this sucker!"

"How do you know all this, sir?" Ozzie asked.

"Come, I'll show you," Nigel said, ushering them into a spacious den with a home theater. They sat down on the couches while the aging explorer rustled through his collection of VHS tapes. "Aha!" he said finally, pulling out an unmarked cassette and popping it in the VCR.

A deleted scene from *Unnatural Wonders* came on the screen. "I had been watching the jellyfish for some time when I first saw the beast," he said as he fast-forwarded the video and pressed Play. "Here."

A shadowy form hovered below the water's surface

and then zipped underneath Nigel's boat. A moment later the sea monster emerged fully out of the water on the other side. Its eel-like body looked more like a sea serpent than a shark, but it was huge, maybe twenty feet long. Its face was dead-eyed and its wide jaw was lined with many rows of razor-sharp teeth.

That thing looks . . . terrifying, Zack thought.

"Yo," cried Rice. "That thing's bigger than the Loch Ness monster!"

"Yeah," Nigel said. "Except this thing is real."

"What are you saying?" Rice scoffed. "That the Loch Ness monster isn't real?"

"Is he kidding?" Nigel said, looking to Zack.

"No," Zack said. "Unfortunately not."

"Nigel," Olivia butted in. "You have to help us find this frilled sea monster."

"I can tell you where a couple of the hot spots for the jellyfish population are located. There's one just off the eastern coast of the Bahamas. And there's a colony that thrives off the southern coast of Jamaica. The giant frilled tiger shark was reported to have been spotted there recently."

"So wait. You're not coming with us?" Madison asked.

"I'm afraid I wouldn't be much good to you." Nigel lifted his pant cuff to reveal a wooden leg. "My adventure days are far behind me."

"Whoa," Rice said. "How'd you lose your leg?"

"Rice, that's not polite to ask," Olivia said.

"No, it's okay," Nigel said. "It was the first time I ever encountered a zombie virus. I was excavating an Egyptian tomb. We found an old coffin in some underground catacombs. When I opened it up, the mummy popped out. I jumped back, but it grabbed me by the leg and bit me right here." He pointed to his shin bone.

"It bit your whole leg off?"

"No," said Nigel. "It just nipped me, but I knew I was infected. So I had to amputate my own leg."

"Cool!" Rice said. "I mean, that's messed up!"

"So you see, I wouldn't be much use out there," he said. "I'd only slow you down. But I'll be here when you get back. That I can assure you.

"I can also lend you my boat. I designed it myself. Now follow me. You'll need a few other things to help you on your mission. . . ." He led them down to the doomsday bunker beneath the main estate and into a room filled with nautical equipment. He grabbed a pair of optical goggles off one of the storage shelves and handed them to Zoe. "Here. These will help you spot the jellyfish. The Turritopsis species is very small and can be hard to locate, but their chemical makeup is quite unique. Through these lenses, the jellyfish will appear bioluminescent and much easier to find."

"What's *bioluminescent*?" Zoe asked.

"In other words," Nigel explained, "when you view them through these goggles, they'll start to glow.

"And take these." Nigel pulled two large harpoon guns off the wall and a leather case full of tranquilizer darts. "When you're ready to capture the frilled shark, hit him with these tranquilizers. Then you can easily reel him in. This way."

They trailed Nigel down a dark, dank hallway and through a doorway that led to an underground cavern that smelled like the sea. As they walked through the island cavern, the cement floor turned to sand, and there was a faint hint of daylight. At the mouth of the cave the Caribbean water shimmered. A wooden dock creaked and swayed on the water's surface.

"There she is," Nigel said. "Isn't she beautiful?"

Nigel's shark-hunting boat rocked back and forth, tethered to the dock. At the stern of the ship, a large fishing crane with a huge reel of steel cable was fashioned to the deck. The pilothouse featured what seemed to be top-of-the-line radar and GPS equipment. A bright fluorescent green pod hung from the starboard side. It had a mechanical crank that raised and lowered it into the water.

"That's a submersible pod, also my own design.
It's a state-of-the-art observation center with turbo
thrusters, LED lights, and a video display that records
underwater expeditions. The lights could come in
handy—the giant frilled tiger shark is attracted to
bright flashing light. There's also a cabin down below,"
Nigel added as he led them on board. "You should all
be able to fit. It's pretty spacious."

Ozzie fiddled with the controls at the steering column. The boat's motor chugged and sputtered, then started to hum. "I think we can take it from here," he said.

"Yeah," Olivia chimed in. "Find the thing. Tranquilize the thing. Reel the thing in. And then bring it back to you, right?"

"Yes," Nigel said. "Are you sure you're up to the task?"

"Don't worry about us," Rice said. "We've got this under control."

We do? Zack thought, unconvinced.

"Very good," Nigel said. "If and when you recover the beast, return here and I'll have everything set up for test trials." He stepped back to shore.

"Nigel," said Zack. "There's one more thing."

"What's that?" Nigel asked.

"We ran into some super zombies out there. I don't think they could have tracked us here, but we can't know for sure. So just be on the lookout. They're not your average zombies, okay?"

"Thank you, Zack. I'll keep an eye out," Nigel said.

"Now go on. You have everything you need to complete this mission. There isn't much time to waste."

"All aboard!" Zoe yelled.

They all waved good-bye to Nigel and hit the high seas in search of the elusive giant frilled tiger shark.

CHAPTER

The sea stretched endlessly in every direction as Zack and Ozzie sailed Nigel's explorer boat toward the Bahamian coast of Exumas. Zack peered out the window, searching the ocean for signs of jellyfish.

Ozzie double-checked the coordinates against Nigel's directions. "This is the place."

"Awesome. I'll go get the others," Zack said, and went to the cabin below.

Rice had fallen asleep, and Madison, Zoe, and Olivia were all standing over him, mischievous grins creeping around their lips. Madison had sprayed a large dollop of shaving cream into the palm of Rice's hand. She stood by his side, filming him on the iPhone. Rice's mouth hung open as he let out an exceptionally loud snore. Olivia covered her mouth, trying not to burst with laughter.

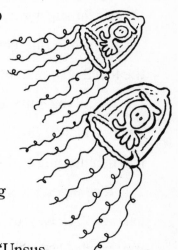

"Welcome to our new show, 'Unsuspecting Victims Unit.' Victim number one: Johnston, Rice." Zoe closed in on Rice, a large bird's feather in her hand primed to tickle his nose.

"What are you guys—" Zack started to say.

WHAP! Rice swatted at the feather and slapped the handful of shaving cream right into his own face. He shot up with a start. The white beard of foam started to slip and reveal a not-so-amused look on his face. "Ha-ha-ha. Very funny. Laugh it up!"

Olivia was on her knees convulsing with silent laughter. "OMG, I can't breathe!"

"Gotcha, sucka!" Zoe pointed at Rice with both hands. "That's for super-zombifying my girl's family!"

"Episode one complete," Madison said, and tapped the touch screen to end the video.

"Will you guys quit messing around?" Zack finally stepped in, handing goggles over to Zoe. "We've got some jellyfish hunting to do."

Rice wiped the shaving cream off his face, and they all followed Zack back up to the main deck. Zoe peered through the goggles Nigel had given them. "I don't see anything."

"They're deep-sea creatures, so maybe we should dive down with the pod," Olivia said.

"Good call, Olivia," Rice said, and went over to unlatch the pod's metal hatch. "Who's coming with me? Zack, you in?"

"Yeah, let's go test this thing out!"

Zack and Rice climbed into the pod's pilot sphere. Inside the steel and acrylic fiberglass chamber, they sat before a panel of touch screen video monitors. An intercom was mounted on the side wall, and a series of vertical and horizontal thruster joysticks were situated on the control panel. An array of beacon lights circled the top of the deep seacraft.

Before they closed the hatch, Twinkles chirruped from the deck and bounded into the sub pod with the boys. "Twinkles, uh-uh," Zack said, but Rice picked up the little pup and placed him on his lap.

"Come on, Zack," said Rice. "Let him come along."

Ozzie hit the mechanized crank, and the submersible pod dropped into the sea with a soft splash.

"Hold it!" Zoe shouted, still looking through the goggles. "I think I just spotted a bunch of jellyfish over there. They're glowing."

Olivia raced to the pilothouse of Nigel's boat and revved the motor.

"Olivia, wait!" Ozzie yelled after her. "Do you know how to steer this thing?"

"Please," she said. "I've known how to sail since I was, like, seven years old." Olivia manned the controls and they

cruised over to the spot, toting Zack and Rice along in the pod. The boat slowed down near a large grouping of tiny jellyfish floating close to the surface.

Zack stared through the high-grade plexi-glass as the pod bobbed through the scores of tiny invertebrates.

"Yo, man," Rice said. "That's definitely them!"

"Are you sure?" Zack asked his buddy.

"You think I don't know what an immortal jellyfish looks like?"

"Okay, guys," Zack spoke back to the boat through the wireless intercom. "These are the jellyfish. Let's get a sample."

Up above, Madison ran to the other side of the boat and grabbed the custom-made microporous fishing net, then leaned over and scooped up a large jellyfish sample. "Got 'em," she said, looking at her catch. "Yuck, they're disgusting!"

"These things shouldn't be at the surface. There must be something scaring them up," Ozzie's voice sounded on the intercom inside the pod. "Maybe it's the giant frilled tiger shark! I'm about to detach the line. You guys go down and try to catch a visual on this frilled shark-a-mabob."

The pod dipped fully underwater, and Ozzie prepared to unhook the line. "Ready?" he asked.

Zack gave him the thumbs-up and they took off.

Zack maneuvered the pod through the water while Rice searched the depths for any sign of life. The water was dark and murky.

Out of the corner of his eye, Zack saw something dart through the cloudy underwater gloom. He squinted to see more clearly. It was two somethings. A pair of zombie barracuda to be exact. Their long thin bodies slithered through the water. The mean-faced fish grimaced with razor-sharp underbites.

BANG! CLANK!

They smashed their pointy snouts against the fiberglass. Three more undead barracudas swam straight for the pod. *BAM! BAM! BAM!*

"Dude, what the heck is going on?" Rice said.

"How did all these fish get zombified?" Zack asked.

"I don't know, man, but there's more coming. . . ."

Two large zombified squid latched onto the glass, soon joined by a foursome of lampreys. The jawless fish sucked at the window with their funnel-like mouths. Their fang-laden lips scratched against the glass like nails on a chalkboard.

More and more zombie sea creatures were quickly piling up against the submersible's fiberglass viewport. Zack and Rice could barely see anything except the pulsating blobs and tentacles pressed up against the window.

"Whoa!" Zack said, glimpsing a dark shape through the mass of undead sea creatures attached to the viewport. "Did you see that?"

"See what?" Rice asked

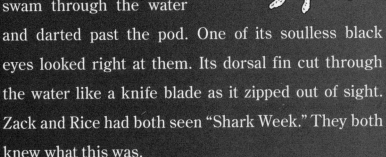

Something huge swam through the water and darted past the pod. One of its soulless black eyes looked right at them. Its dorsal fin cut through the water like a knife blade as it zipped out of sight. Zack and Rice had both seen "Shark Week." They both knew what this was.

"Dude," said Rice. "It's zombie Jaws!"

"He must have scared up the jellyfish," Zack said, and then lifted the intercom to his mouth. "No go, Oz!" he said. "We need to come back up—now!"

The zombified great white shark appeared again as a blurry shadow.

"What's the problem,

Zack?" Ozzie's voice came over the speakers.

"We got a visual," Zack said. "But it's the wrong kind of shark."

The great white's shadow grew closer and closer, swimming full throttle. Zack's eyes went wide as it bee-lined for the pod.

"Brace yourself!" Zack shouted.

"Hmm, hmm . . . ," Twinkles whimpered.

The shark smashed its pointed snout into the rounded glass. *POW!*

A large crack split down the interior of the window.

"Rice, we have to get back to the surface," Zack said. "This thing's not going to be able to take the pressure!"

"Abort mission!" Rice shouted into the intercom. "I repeat, abort mission!" But there was only the sound of crackling static on the other end. "Bring us up, Zack!"

"Something's wrong," Zack said, trying to move the joystick. "The thrusters aren't working!"

"Look," Rice said, and pointed to an emergency but-ton on the control panel. "I think we might be able to activate the turbo-boosters and get back up."

The undead shark circled them again as it prepared to take another crack at their pod.

"Come on, man!" Rice shouted. "Hurry!"

Zack pressed the button, and the pod charged upward. As they ascended to the surface of the Caribbean, the cracking porthole began to leak and water started filling up around their feet.

"Get us out of here!" Rice screamed.

Above them, Madison and Ozzie reconnected the cord from Nigel's ship to the pod. Ozzie tried to pull open the hatch to let Zack and Rice out, but the latch was stuck.

Zack looked back out at the water. The zombified

great white raced toward them. Just as Zack braced for impact, he felt a sudden jerk. The pod lifted out of the water, and the shark missed its target, speeding underneath them.

Rice opened the hatch and scrambled out. Zack grabbed Twinkles in one arm and climbed up through the hatch, one-handed. He could see the shark's form swim eerily and ominously beneath them. A sharp twinge of fear rushed through him as he wobbled on top of the pod, about to step back onto the boat. As he was about to hand Twinkles to Rice, a powerful thud rocked them.

"Whoa!" Zack struggled to keep his balance.

KERTWANG! The great white lurched out of the ocean and clashed its teeth against the welded metal of the pod.

Zack lost his footing and flew back, losing hold of Twinkles. The little dog woofed and went flying bug-eyed through the air, splashing into the churning whirlpool of undead sea creatures below.

"Twinkles!" Madison screeched as Zack managed to get back on the boat.

"Look what you did, Zack!" Zoe cried.

"I didn't mean to!" Zack shouted. "I thought you had him!"

"Me?" Rice yelled. "You weren't even mid-handoff, dude!"

Down below, Twinkles doggy-paddled around, barking like mad. Fifteen yards away, the zombie shark's dorsal fin rose out of the water and then disappeared back beneath the surface.

"Well, somebody go back in there and save him!" Madison shouted.

"Are you kidding me?" Zack said. "There's a great white shark in there."

"Get the net, dum-dums," Ozzie said over the sound of their bickering.

"Good idea, Ozzie." Olivia hurried across the deck. She picked up the net full of jellyfish specimens and dumped them out into a bucket. "Here!" she said, and heaved the fishing net at Madison, who caught it with both hands.

"Twinkles!" Madison yelled down to her pup. She leaned as far as she could over the railing, trying to angle the net to scoop up Twinkles.

"Arf! Arf!" the little Boggle yelped helplessly.

A dull thunk sounded underneath them as something nudged the starboard side of the boat. Madison nearly dropped the fishing net as the boat rocked them all off balance.

"There! Got him!" Madison grunted, netting the little canine and pulling him in. The water swirled and roiled beneath the little dog. *VROOSH!* The great white leaped out of the ocean, its massive undead jaws wide open, primed to chomp the entire net clean in half.

"Ahhhh!" Madison shouted, and yanked back. She

hoisted the fishing net upward as the shark's jaw snapped shut with an awful clack.

"Arf! Arf!" Twinkles yowled as the great white's teeth barely missed him. Madison slipped and fell back on her tailbone, dropping the net. Twinkles hit the deck safely aboard the boat.

"Yeah!" they all yelled. "Woo-hoo!"

"Take that, you stupid shark!" Olivia pumped her fist. "No puppy snacks today!"

"Everyone okay?" Zack asked as his pulsing heart rate slowed down a bit.

They were all fine, including Twinkles. Madison lifted the little dog from the boat deck and cuddled him in her arms. Twinkles whimpered and trembled as they all huddled up.

"Okay, guys," Ozzie said. "We need a new plan."

"Yeah, these waters are completely infested," Zack said. "If there is a giant frilled tiger shark around here, then it may already be zombified."

Olivia pointed to the chum bucket filled with the immortal jellyfish sample. "Didn't Nigel say there was a ton of those things down near Jamaica?"

"Yes," said Rice. "And there was supposedly a frilled tiger shark sighting there, too!"

"Jamaica it is, then," Zack said.

"Yah, mon!" Zoe said in a bad Caribbean accent. "Jamaica, mon!"

Ozzie furrowed his eyebrows at her. "All in favor of Zoe never doing that voice ever again raise your hand."

They all put up their hands except for Zoe.

CHAPTER 8

On the way to Jamaica, the waves began to slop against the sides of the boat. The sky overhead took on a dark, ominous hue as thick storm clouds rolled in. A flash of lightning flickered in the distance.

"Looks like we're hitting some rocky waters," Ozzie said as their boat rose and plunged through the choppy waves.

"Yeah," said Madison. "You guys want to head belowdeck? I think I'm starting to get a little seasick."

"Me, too," said Zoe, whose face had turned a pale shade of green. "I need to lie down."

"Where's Rice?" Zack asked.

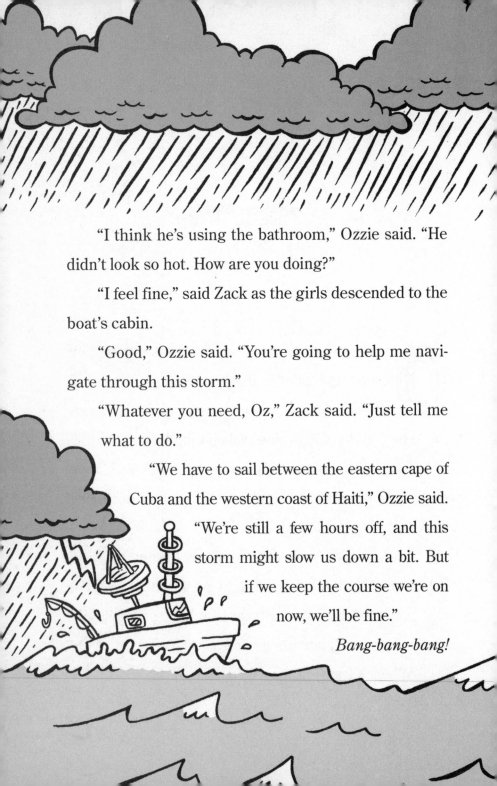

"I think he's using the bathroom," Ozzie said. "He didn't look so hot. How are you doing?"

"I feel fine," said Zack as the girls descended to the boat's cabin.

"Good," Ozzie said. "You're going to help me navigate through this storm."

"Whatever you need, Oz," Zack said. "Just tell me what to do."

"We have to sail between the eastern cape of Cuba and the western coast of Haiti," Ozzie said. "We're still a few hours off, and this storm might slow us down a bit. But if we keep the course we're on now, we'll be fine."

Bang-bang-bang!

Someone knocked loudly downstairs, and they heard a muffled yell through the deck. "Rice, get out of there! I'm gonna be sick!"

The cabin door leading belowdeck swung open with a bang, and Rice barreled through it. Zack's friend was off balance, struggling to stay upright as he raced to the port side of the rollicking vessel.

"Dude, what are you doing?" Zack said. "Get back inside!"

"We're all seasick." Rice groaned. "And Olivia just kicked me out of the bathroom!"

"Yeah," Zack said. "Zoe does that to me all the time."

"Hoooghlargh!" Rice retched and heaved over the side, spewing his last cruise ship meal into the stormy sea.

Now Zoe stormed up from belowdeck and sprinted to the boat's side rail. Madison ran up after her. Her cheeks puffed out like a blowfish as she covered her mouth with one hand.

"Blaaahhh!" A long stream of rancid vomit sprayed all over the deck of their boat.

A pained look came over Ozzie's face. "Uh-oh," he said.

"What's the matter?" Zack asked. "Don't tell me you're seasick, too."

"I don't get seasick," Ozzie said, doubling over. "I just can't stand seeing other people throw up. . . ."

It makes me have to throw up." Ozzie started to run out of the pilothouse clutching his stomach.

"Wait a second," Zack said. "Who's going to steer the boat?"

"Aarghh!" Ozzie groaned. "Just keep us on course. It's easy."

I hope Ozzie's right, Zack thought as he stared into the turbulent sea and the dark storm up ahead. *Because I have no idea what I'm doing.*

Nigel's boat rocked in the swell of the waves. Zack checked the GPS screen at the steering column. They were still on the proper course, but Zack grew nervous as the storm worsened. The wind howled menacingly and whipped huge torrents of rain against the windows of the pilothouse, making it difficult to see.

"Phloooorrghph!" Rice retched again and spewed stomach bile into the wind. Zack cringed as the projectile vomit flew back into Zoe's face. She slugged Rice in the belly, and he puked again, this time at his own feet.

The boat tipped up over the crest of a massive wave and plunged down on the other side with a mighty splash. The boat jostled, and salt water sprayed over the railings onto the deck. The boat rocked again, and Zack pitched backward into the control panel inside the pilothouse.

The boat's course shifted on the stormy sea. Zack stuck his head out in the pelting wind and called down to Ozzie, "Hey, man, we got thrown off course. What do I do?" But he got no answer. His friends were in the throes of their seasickness, too busy hurling bellies full of vomit over the side to respond.

Zack turned back to the dark, violent ocean ahead of them. He couldn't see through the wind and rain. A bright flash of lightning cracked across the sky and illuminated the area around them.

Zack gasped at what he saw. A rocky island coastline appeared straight ahead of them. He took to the steering controls while the island grew closer and closer. Zack tried to maneuver the boat off the collision course, but it couldn't gain a wide enough berth to avoid the inevitable.

A horrible snapping sound rang out as they scraped over what must have been a shallow coral reef.

The boat jerked and flung Zack sidelong into the rail with a clunk. His head stung and started to throb. The boat rode into the sandy banks and halted in the shallow water.

CHAPTER

The downpour became a mere drizzle as their shipwreck floated toward the white sandy beach of the unknown island.

"Aw, man . . . ," Zack said. He rose to his feet slowly and exited the pilothouse. He rubbed his head. He could feel a goose egg–sized bump forming above his brow. He looked at his friends sprawled out across the deck. "You guys all right?"

"If by all right you mean it feels like a dozen microscopic zombies are nibbling away at my intestines, then yeah, I'm all right," Rice said.

"Ugh!" Madison groaned. "Why did you have to say

that? Now I'm imagining a dozen zombie microbes eating away at my intestines!"

"What just happened?" Olivia said, coming up from the cabin. Her hair looked like she'd just brushed it with a rabid squirrel.

"Zack crashed the boat." Madison groaned, still clutching her tummy.

"Don't blame me," Zack snapped. "If you guys hadn't been puking your guts out, Ozzie wouldn't have gotten sick."

"Oh, so now it's my fault?" Madison asked.

"Don't worry, Madison," Zoe said. "Zack just likes to pretend he's not a total screwup sometimes, which we all know isn't true."

"Shut up, Zoe!" said Zack. "Why don't you go look in a mirror and try not to throw up some more?"

"Ha!" Rice laughed. "Good luck with that!"

"Rice," said Zoe, "don't you have some zombie sharks to go swimming with?"

"Guys!" Olivia shouted. "This is no time to be bickering. Our boat is seriously messed up."

"She's right," Ozzie said. "This isn't looking too good."

They all peered over the stern. The propeller was bent beyond repair, it seemed, and there was a sizable hole in the front of the boat. "Hoooglargh!" Rice moaned and spewed one last mouthful of throw up onto the deck.

Ozzie clutched his stomach and heaved up another bellyful of vomit. "You really need to stop that, bro."

"Sorry," Rice said.

"What are we supposed to do now?" Zack said, thinking out loud.

Ozzie stood up despite the pain in his abdomen. "All we can do, man."

"Which is what exactly?" Zoe asked.

"Get to shore. Find some sort of shelter. Locate a food source and then hopefully find something to patch up this boat with."

They climbed the ladder to the sand dune and waded to the shoreline. The six of them and Twinkles plopped down on the beach and sighed, exhausted and dejected.

"This is totally wack," said Rice, groaning as he lay back on the sand. "How the heck are we supposed to

track down the frilled tiger shark without Nigel's boat?"

"Okay," Madison whined. "I'm ready to go home now."

"Come on, guys," Zack said. "I know you're all sick and tired, but we can't give up. There's no one else who can save the world from these zombies."

"Zack's right," Olivia said. "We have to get back out there so we can take down these super zombies once and for all!"

"That's the spirit," Ozzie said as he rose to his feet. "Who knows anything about wildlife vegetation?"

"I do," Olivia said. "I used to go camping a lot with my dad."

"Good," Ozzie said. "We'll gather up as many edible plants and fruits as we can. Twinkles, you stay with us." The little pup sat obediently at Ozzie's heels. Ozzie turned to Zack, Zoe, Madison, and Rice. "You four go on an expedition and see what's on the other side of the island."

"Oh yeah," Zoe said. "That sounds real fair. You two go berry picking and we get to go hiking through some tropical island jungle."

"Come on," Zack said to his sister. "There are four of us. We'll be fine. Plus we need to see if there's anyone here who can help us patch up the boat."

"Yeah, Zoe, let's go," said Madison. "Maybe there's a town or something on the other side."

"Only one way to find out." Zack led the way through the tropical forest, using his baseball bat to hack through the thick island vegetation. Rice, Zoe, and Madison all carried the golf clubs they had taken from the cruise ship before they left.

As they trekked through the dense greenery, Zack paused and shushed the rest of the group. "Why are we stopping?" Madison asked.

"And please don't shush me again," Zoe said. "You know I don't like to be shushed."

"Shhhh!" Zack shushed her again. "Listen."

A strange animalistic noise rustled in the leafy bracken beside them.

"Sounded like something growling," Rice said.

"Are there tigers or leopards out here?" Zoe asked.

"Zombies are one thing, but we won't stand a chance against a jungle cat with just golf clubs and a baseball bat."

"Actually, we should probably be more worried about poisonous spiders and snakes in this region," Rice

said in a smart-alecky voice.

"Thanks for that, Rice," said Madison. "That's very comforting."

"Just sayin'," Rice said, shrugging his shoulders. Pushing deeper into the island jungle, they hopped over

twisted, knobby roots and batted away the dark green foliage.

"This way, guys," Zack said. "It looks like there's something up ahead."

They picked up the pace and then slowed as they reached a clearing in the tropical forest. Zack's eyes roamed over the terrain and fell on a narrow dirt path imprinted with tire tracks.

"Let's follow it," Madison said. "There's got to be someone who can help us."

They plodded down the dirt road, looking for any signs of life. But besides the tire tracks, there was nothing, not even a footprint. They kept walking until Zack stopped dead in his tracks. A low rumble sounded up ahead of them.

"What is that?" Rice asked.

"I don't know," said Zack.

"Let's go look, then, you little dweeb-meisters," said Zoe, and took the lead from the boys.

As they continued down the road, the dull rumble became more of a mechanical roar. They approached two large generators feeding electricity to some sort of work shed. Zack opened the door and looked in. The place was filled with all kinds of carpentry and iron-welding tools. Various cuts of lumber and scrap metal were piled next to the shed.

"Looks like somebody must live here," Zack said. "Let's keep going."

A little farther on, they found two gigantic trees with huge twisting branches. One of the tree trunks had a wooden staircase spiraling up to where an elaborate tree house was built into the branches.

"Holy moly," Rice said. "It's a giant tree fort!"

"Oh no," Madison said to Zoe. "Please tell me we haven't died and gone to nerd heaven!"

"Come on," Zack said, walking toward the structure. "Whoever made this thing is probably pretty handy. Let's see if they're home."

The four of them walked up the steep spiral staircase, which led to a wooden platform. A rope bridge hung between two huge branches and led to a bunch of wooden huts in the treetops.

"Hello!" Rice called out as they walked across the rope bridge. "Anybody home?"

Nobody answered.

"All right," Zack said. "Madison and I will check those two huts to the left. Rice, you and Zoe go check that big shack over there." Zack followed Madison across a shorter, more rickety rope bridge and crept cautiously inside

the tree house hut. The door creaked on its hinges as they both stepped inside. The room was empty except for a bed and a small dresser with a mirror above it.

"Nothing much here," Madison said, peering inside the drawers. They made their way to the next hut, constructed on the adjacent tree branch.

It was another

bedroom with a king-size bed at the center. Zack and Madison paused in the middle of the room, looking around. The mirror on the back of the door was shattered and a spot of what looked like blood dribbled down the glass.

"Yuck," she said. "Something definitely gross happened here."

Zack checked out the bloody mirror and then wandered across the room. He picked up a framed photograph off the nightstand.

"What's that?" Madison asked as she closed the door behind her.

"Family photo or something," Zack said. He was looking at a picture of a brother, a sister, a mom, and a dad. He stared at the photograph for a long moment. It reminded him of his own family, and suddenly all he wanted was for things to get back to normal. Just good times and family dinners, even if that did include Zoe tormenting him mercilessly. In a weird way, he missed even that.

"Zack," Madison said. "Zack!"

"What?" Zack said, putting the photograph back on the dresser.

"I just heard something. . . ."

They both listened and heard the creak of the rope bridge right outside the door.

"Rice!" Zack hollered. "Zoe?" But no one answered.

In the distance, Zoe and Rice let out a double shriek that rang out through the treetops.

"Come on!" Zack shouted, and both he and Madison raced across the bedroom to go help their friends. *WHAM!* The door flung open and blasted both Zack and Madison back into the bedroom. Madison stumbled into the dresser with a bang. Zack flew to the floor, his bat rolling underneath the bed. He looked back over his shoulder at the gruesome beast in the doorway. It resembled the brother from the photograph, except that this dude was zombified.

The thing's face was an absolute nightmare. The brother zombie clacked its black-rotted choppers in an endless series of quick, chattering chomps. Bits of enamel and other toothy shrapnel exploded out of its mouth. The undead hooligan grunted and shot two snot rockets the color of mint jelly from its nostrils. They landed with a splat on the floor near Zack's feet.

The brother zombie took a thunderous step forward. It was a pretty big guy, maybe seventeen years old. Zack needed to get his bat for this fella. He reached under the bed and stretched his fingertips to grab the wooden handle.

Madison charged toward the zombie with her golf club. But as she planted her feet to swing the club, she slipped on the blob of lime green slime the beast had just ejected.

"Ahhhh!" Madison screamed as she hit the floor and the zombie jumped on top of her. "Help!"

Zack grabbed the baseball bat and dragged it out from under the bed. He hopped to his feet and raised the bat over the zombie's head. He clobbered the undead brute on the back of its skull. The zombie fell with a thud and slumped limply on the floor.

Zack breathed a sigh of relief as Madison picked herself up and brushed herself off. The unconscious zombie lay on the ground in front of them. "You all good?" Zack asked her.

"Think so," Madison said. "You?"

"Uh-huh," he said.

"Help!" Rice shouted from outside. "We got problems!"

CHAPTER

Z ack and Madison rushed out of the tree house bedroom to help their friends.

The clan of deserted island zombies had Rice and Zoe trapped in the middle of the rope bridge. The mom and dad were on one side. Their daughter and their undead dog hobbled on the other, cutting off their only escape route.

"You guys, help us!" Zoe screamed. "We're about to get our brains eaten by Swiss Family Zombison!"

"Save yourself, Zoe. If you walk right past them, they probably won't attack you," Rice said. "Because you have no brains."

Zoe and Rice had their clubs poised to swing as they went back to back, each of them facing a pair of rezombified tree people. The family's zombified dog stalked toward them slowly. It bared its fangs and frothed at the mouth while panting vigorously.

Mr. and Mrs. Zombison staggered unsteadily toward Zoe. Their stiff-limbed walks made the rope bridge wobble. On the opposite side, the daughter raised its hands into sharp little claws, fingernails red with blood and dirt.

Zack looked around. There was no way they could make a jump for it. They were up way too high.

"Rice, quick! Unzombify them," Zack said. "Give them the gumball antidote."

"But we don't have that many left, man," Rice said.

"What if we need them later?"

"Maybe they can help us fix the boat," Zack said.

"Yeah, but what if we unzombify them and they turn out to be even bigger psychos than their zombie selves?" Rice said. "I mean, who lives all alone on an island? Psychos, that's who."

"I'm about to go psycho on you if you don't unzom-bify these freaks," Zoe said.

"For real," Madison said to Zack. "That dog's bug-ging me out."

The zombie dog growled hideously, now only a few feet from Rice.

"Okay, okay," Rice said, and placed two gumballs on the wooden slats of the rope bridge. Rice handed Zoe two and she placed them in similar fashion in front of the rezombified parents.

The zombie dog went for one of the gumballs and gobbled it up. A moment later it dropped in a heap on the wooden slats of the rope bridge.

Mr. and Mrs. Zombison each grabbed one of the gumballs off the rope bridge. The Zombisons' daughter dove onto the bridge, picked up one of the gumballs, and shoveled it into its mouth.

"Braiiiins!" the girl intoned in a dreadfully demonic voice, chewing with her mouth wide open.

She swallowed the gumball, and all three Zombisons keeled over face-first. The rope bridge swayed dangerously side to side. Zoe and Rice both held on to the side rails for balance until the swinging stopped.

"What about big bro back in the hut?" Zack said.

"I'll go take care of it," said Madison. She bounded across the rope bridge to unzombify the brother Zombison.

"Okay," Zack said. "We'll get the rest of these guys off the rope bridge and into the tree house."

Shortly after the Zombisons had shaken off their zombification, they sat across from Zack, Rice, Zoe, and Madison in the main tree house. The whole family looked very confused.

"So how did you guys get zombified, exactly?" Madison asked.

"I have no idea," the father said. "I don't remember much."

"The last thing I remember was doing the dishes after dinner. I must have blacked out," said the mother.

"Sounds like you guys got rezombified," Rice said. "You're from the U.S.?"

"Bob Smith," the father said. "Cleveland, Ohio. This is my wife, Melanie. And this is our son, Jim, and our daughter, Laura."

"We were all zombified in the first BurgerDog outbreak," Mrs. Smith added. "Once we were unzombified by the popcorn antidote, we decided as a family to live on an island so that in the event of another zombie apocalypse, we would be safe. I guess we were wrong."

"What do you mean when you say . . . rezombified?" Laura asked.

"The popcorn antidote from the first outbreak wore off after six months," Zack told them. "Everyone cured from the first outbreak just up and rezombified."

"How do you guys know all this?" asked Mr. Smith.

"Wait a second," Laura said. "We know you guys!" She turned to her brother. "These are the kids who saved everyone during the first zombie outbreak."

The whole family's eyes widened.

"So it is," said Mr. Smith. "What do you know."

"It's true, it is us," Rice said proudly. "And if you guys have a pen, I'll be happy to sign an autograph for you."

Zack nudged Rice in the ribs with his elbow.

"Don't mind him," Madison said. "He's kind of a moron."

"Where is your other friend?" Laura asked. "Weren't there five of you?"

"Ozzie Briggs," Rice said. "He's gathering up food down on the beach."

"Yeah, he's with Olivia," said Madison. "She's my cousin and also the zombie antidote now."

"But I thought you were?" Laura said.

"It's a long story," said Madison.

"So you kids are off saving the world again, huh?" Mr. Smith said. "If you're all the way out here unzombifying us, then you must have saved everybody back home already, right?"

"Unfortunately, no," Zack said. "It's still pretty bad out there. We actually got shipwrecked on your island a few hours ago. Is there any way you could take a look at our boat and see if there's any way to patch things up?"

"Anything for you kids," Mrs. Smith said. "Bob's a pretty handy guy."

"Of course I'll take a look," Mr. Smith said. "Can't make any promises, but let's go check it out."

When they got back to the beach, Zack called out to Ozzie and Olivia, who were still busy gathering food. "Hey, guys! Come over and meet the Smiths! They live on the island."

Mr. Smith followed Ozzie and Zack out to Nigel's shipwrecked boat and inspected the damage.

Mr. Smith scratched his head. "Hmm, I don't know. This sucker's pretty dinged up."

"Dang it!" Zack kicked the wet sand with a splash, showing his frustration.

"Now hold on," Mr. Smith continued. "We've got an

extra motor boat on the other side of the island. You're welcome to take that if you want."

"I'm afraid that's not going to work, sir," Ozzie explained. "This is a specially designed shark-hunting boat. If we're going to track down the giant frilled tiger shark and reverse the super zombie virus strain, then it's gotta be this boat right here."

"Hmm, sounds pretty fancy. Let's see if we can't salvage this thing." Mr. Smith thought for a moment and then called to his son. "Jimbo, come have a look-see!"

Jim jogged across the beach and waded out to the sand dune. "Oooh," he said, checking out the damage for himself. "That's messed up! Busted rudder. The engine's been punctured. And you got a hole in the keel."

"Think that spare motor would work on this?" Mr. Smith asked him.

Jim scratched his chin thoughtfully. "Maybe. We can definitely try it."

"Then why don't we all go back to the house and grab some tools and wood," he said. "You can start patching up that hole while I work on the motor."

"Sounds good, Pops," Jim said.

While the Smith men worked on Nigel's boat, Ozzie took to fashioning himself another set of nunchaku. He had found two suitable pieces of wood, a chain, and two metal hooks. It didn't take long before his new martial arts weapon of choice was complete and he was testing it out on the beach, taking down invisible zombies move after move.

Rice and Zack played fetch with Twinkles and the Smiths' unzombified dog, Bruno. The girls hung out with

Laura drinking lemonade Mrs. Smith had brought from the house.

By the time Jim and his father had patched up the hole and replaced the motor, the sun had sunk to just above the horizon of the ocean.

"Thank you so much for all your help," Zack told Mr. Smith and his son. "Now we've got to hit the road. I mean the water."

"Are you sure you have to go back out there?" Laura asked. "It's so dangerous."

"You're welcome to stay here with us," Mr. Smith said, "until things blow over."

"Thanks," said Zack. "But things aren't going to blow over unless we do the huffing and puffing."

"Yeah," Rice said. "We have to hunt down this giant shark or else we may never be able to make a super zombie antidote."

"Well, at the very least you can all stay for dinner," Mrs. Smith said. "I was thinking about making lasagna."

"I'd love to stay and have a home-cooked meal," said Olivia, "but I seriously doubt you guys have vegan cheese on the island."

"No," Mrs. Smith said. "But I could make you a salad if you want."

The kids all looked at one another. They knew they could all use a home-cooked meal. "We're in," Rice said, rubbing his tummy.

"Okay." Mrs. Smith smiled. "It's the least we can do to thank you for unzombifying us."

Within the hour, the six of them plus the Smith

family had devoured three huge lasagnas and two big bowls of fresh salad.

"Thanks, Mrs. S," said Zack. "That was amazing!"

"You're welcome," she said. "Anything to help you guys complete your mission."

There was an awkward pause at the dinner table, then Laura spoke up. "We're not going to rezombify again, are we?"

"There's no reason you should this time," Rice said. "I made those gumballs myself."

"That's a relief." Mrs. Smith sighed.

"Well," Ozzie said, tossing his napkin on the table. "Hate to eat and run, but we need to get going."

"We understand," said Mr. Smith. "Thank you for saving us."

The Smith family walked the kids back down to the beach and waved good-bye. With his belly stuffed with lasagna, Zack felt good and full, like when he used to lie on the couch after a family dinner. "If you ever need a place to stay, don't hesitate to stop by," Mr. Smith called to them as the kids waded out to the boat.

"Thanks again for dinner!" Olivia yelled back.

"Good luck saving the world!" Laura shouted to them.

"Thanks!" Zack called back. "We're going to need it!"

The troller boat's new motor growled, and they zipped off into the dark Caribbean night.

ack at sea, Zack and Olivia were on night watch, sailing quietly through the now calm Caribbean night. Zack gazed pensively out at the black, star-speckled sky and the vast ocean before them.

"Hey, chatterbox." Olivia broke the silence. "What are you thinking about?"

"Actually," he said, "I'm kind of trying not to think right now."

"Why's that?"

"I don't know," he said. "All I can think about is how bad we messed things up and now it might never be okay again."

"No point thinking like that," she said. "Probably

good to turn your brain off for a while. You want to see a magic trick?"

"Sure," Zack said. He was always up for a little magic. "Do you know one?"

"A couple," she said, pulling out a brand-new deck of cards and peeling off the plastic wrapper.

"Where'd you get those?" Zack asked.

"I snagged a deck back on the cruise ship."

"Nice," Zack said.

Olivia cracked the cards open and gave them a few shuffles. "Pick a card, any card," she said, fanning them out.

Zack reached for one. "Not that one," Olivia said sternly, and Zack paused, furrowing his brow. "Just kidding." She smiled. "Pick whichever one you want."

Zack picked a queen of hearts and then put it back in the deck.

Olivia shuffled the cards again, and Zack cut the stack for good measure. She held the deck to her forehead. "Okay, now think of your card," she said. Zack closed his eyes and pictured the card. "You're not thinking hard enough."

"Yes I am," Zack protested.

"Touchy, touchy." Olivia smirked. She took the deck and smacked it into the palm of her hand three times before tossing the cards onto the floor. They all scattered faceup except for a single card that landed facedown. She gestured for Zack to pick it up.

He flipped the card over. "Queen of hearts," he said. "That's my card!"

"I know," Olivia said, taking a slight bow. "Pretty cool, eh?"

"How'd you do that?"

 "A magician never tells her secrets. . . ." She paused and swallowed hard. "My dad taught that one to me. Whenever my brother and I were sick or down in the dumps, he always used to cheer us up with one of his card tricks."

"He sounds like a good dad," Zack said.

"Yeah." Olivia looked away. "Hard to believe that he's some deranged, undead super psycho."

"I know," Zack said. "My parents are zombies right now, too."

 "I've never been this scared in my life," she said.

"Me neither," said Zack. "But listen, we're going to figure out a way to get everything back the way it was. I promise."

Zack knew he shouldn't make promises he couldn't keep, but Olivia smiled, so it was worth it.

Zack's eyes flicked open at first light. Olivia was passed out, snoring on the boat's wooden bench. The wind had blown the playing cards all over the deck.

Zack stretched a crick out of his neck and yawned loudly. Olivia stirred and mumbled something incoherent, then continued to snooze. It was still dark out despite the faint pink glow of dawn peeking over the horizon.

Zack looked out across the water. They were cruising along the southern coast of a large land mass.

"Is that—?" Olivia said, lifting her head out of slumber.

"I think so. Hold on, I want to make sure," Zack said. He ran up to the control room and checked the GPS to confirm. It was Jamaica.

He gave Olivia the thumbs-up then rushed to tell the others. "Wake up, guys," Zack said, poking his head down in the cabin, where everyone was sprawled out in various sleeping postures. "We made it!"

Rice spoke without opening his eyes. "Good job."

Ozzie shot up in his seat and looked around disoriented. "What happened?"

"We're here, Oz," Zack said. "Everybody, get up. We got work to do."

They slowed their boat to a crawl a ways off the coastline of Port Royal. Zack peered through the binoculars, looking onto the large island's southern shore. Hundreds upon hundreds of undead Jamaican islanders were milling around the coastline, waddling into the ocean. The whole island had an eerie orange glow. Enormous, dense gray tendrils of smoke wafted skyward from the fires that raged inland.

"We have to start looking for the frilled shark quick," Olivia said. "And then get the heck out of here before this whole place gets zombified."

"What are we going to do?" Zack asked.

"First, we're going to need some more bait," Olivia said. "Nigel said that there was a massive colony of those jellyfish around here."

"And where there are jellyfish, there could be a giant frilled tiger shark," said Rice, pulling out the jellyfish spotting goggles Nigel had given them.

"You see anything, Rice?" Ozzie asked, steering the boat away from port.

"Out there." Rice pointed southwest. "I think I see the colony."

The boat cruised out about a half mile from the shoreline and drifted into the humongous colony of immortal jellyfish.

Olivia picked up the specially designed fishing net, leaned over the side of the boat, and ran it through the water. She scooped as many of the little jellyfish as she could reach with the net. She then dumped them in with the jellyfish from before, filling the chum bucket to the brim.

"How are we going to bait the hook?" Ozzie asked, running his hands through the bucket of minuscule jellyfish. "They're so small."

"I have an idea," Olivia said. "Can I borrow your survival knife?"

Ozzie handed her the blade and she sliced the microporous material away from the rim of the net. Olivia dipped the net in the bucket and scooped up some of the jellyfish. She tied off the top of the net and held up the pouch. "If this thing lives down so deep, then we ought to send him a little treat and try to lure him up," Olivia said. "Or maybe just catch us one big old fiz-nish."

She baited the hook on the fishing pole crane with the net full of jellyfish and sent it down. She turned to Madison and Zoe. "You guys keep an eye on that and see if we get a bite."

With the bait dangling a few leagues under the sea, they trolled the Jamaican waters.

"All we can really do is wait, I guess," Zack said, watching the fishing line intently.

"That's not all we can do," Ozzie said, walking over to the submersible pod on board. "I think it's time to take this bad boy for another spin."

"What do you expect to do with that?" Zoe said. "We can't go down in that thing again."

"Yeah," said Rice. "But didn't Nigel say that the frilled shark is attracted to light?"

"That's right," Olivia said. "If we flash the lights on the pod, maybe we can lure it up!"

"Then me and Oz can harpoon the sucker!" Rice sounded excited.

Zack, Madison, and Olivia ran over to the pod. Zack flicked on the lights

while Madison and Olivia unhooked it from the cable and lowered the pod into the water near the baited jellyfish hook. They watched as the pod illuminated the murky depths below their boat in a pale, dull glow.

Now all they could do was wait.

"Rice, get ready. You and I will man the harpoon guns in case the frilled shark rises to the surface," Ozzie said. Ozzie and Rice loaded the harpoon guns in preparation for the biggest catch of their lives.

"Ugh, how long is this going to take?" Zoe complained, obviously not enjoying the fishing experience.

"Look!" Madison shouted to everyone, and pointed off the port side of their boat. The water around the baited net full of jellyfish stirred and started to rotate like a whirlpool.

They all peered over the side of the boat.

The outline of something humongous jetted through the light and then zipped into the shadows. It looked like some kind of giant eel, well over fifteen feet long. Zack recognized the shape of the sea creature from Nigel's video.

"It's the giant frilled tiger shark!"

oly mackerel!" Rice shouted. "Look at the size of it!"

Madison squealed as the massive, prehistoric sea beast reared its head out of the water. "Ew! It's so nasty looking!"

The giant frilled tiger shark wrenched its long flexible jaws open wide. It lunged toward the jellyfish bait with the quickness of a serpent. *CHOMP!* One mighty bite and the net of immortal jellyfish disappeared.

The gigantic fish snagged on the large metal hook and rocked the boat with its massive weight.

"Hurry up, Rice!" Ozzie yelled from behind the harpoon gun turret. He lined up the sea creature in his sight. Rice peered down the barrel of his harpoon gun. They both pulled their triggers at the same time. Two tranquilizers flew through the Caribbean dawn and sank into the giant frilled tiger shark's topskin. *THUNK-THUNK!*

The rare deep-sea dweller let out a ferocious noise and thrashed violently in the water. The harpoons tugged at the frilled shark's flesh, nearly ripping out two big chunks of its skin.

"It's going to break away!" Ozzie yelled to Rice. "Give it some slack!"

The two boys both stopped cranking and allowed the beast to swim out a bit.

The sea monster's thrashing slowly turned into a weak wriggle. Before long the giant frilled tiger shark became docile from the heavy-duty tranquilizer darts.

"We got him!" Rice shouted. The rare sea shark hung limply from the rope lines.

"Open the cage so we can reel it in all the way!" Ozzie yelled.

Zoe ran to the pilothouse and

pulled the lever to open the special underwater compartment. Ozzie and Rice hauled the massive fish belowdeck. Zack raced toward them and high-fived his buddies. "Yeah, baby!"

"Nice shooting, boys," Madison said. "But we got bigger fish to fry."

"I don't know, Madison," Rice said. "This one's pretty gigantic. . . . What the—"

HONK! HONK! Two loud, familiar horns tooted in the distance. Zack's stomach dropped.

The *Fun World* cruise ship sailed toward them, captained by Cousin Ben and his goon squad of super zombies. *Oh no*, Zack thought, *they hijacked the cruise ship! That means they found Nigel's island.* Zack prayed that Nigel's fortress had withstood the super zombie attack. Or else they'd be in even more trouble than they already were.

"This could get messy," Ozzie said, cracking his knuckles.

He steered their boat out of the way of the oncoming super zombie cruise ship. A minute later and the massive megaship would have plowed their much smaller boat to bits.

As they gazed up, trying to see what was going on, three super zombies hurled themselves over the rails of the cruise ship and landed on the deck of their boat. *Thump-thump-thump!*

The kids all grabbed their hand weapons and turned to face the super zombie trio. For a moment, nobody twitched a muscle. The super zombies ogled the kids with their cold, googly eyes.

Behind them, Bunco's cruise ship sailed full steam into port and crashed into the harbor, stranding the remaining super zombies on the Jamaican beach.

"Aaarrghle!" The tallest of the super zombies gargled phlegm in the back of its throat and lurched toward them.

Rice wound up his golf club and swung right at the super zombie's head. But the zombie pirate anticipated the move. Catching the putter in one undead hand, it ripped it away from Rice. It then took the golf club in both hands, bent the metal handle, and chucked it overboard.

"Whoa," Rice said, empty-handed. "Not cool."

Zack and Zoe circled the super zombie woman. Zack clutched his baseball bat firmly as the insane zombie freak hissed and snarled at them. He took a swing and blasted the undead lady in the ribs. The super zombie squawked and growled. It got a running start and then leaped at Zack, but Zoe picked up the pole they'd clipped the net from and hooked the super ghoul around the neck like a dogcatcher. She yanked back hard, and the super zombie dropped flat on the deck of the ship.

To the right of them, Ozzie pulled out his newly made nunchaku and set his sights on the muscular super zombie. Ozzie spun and whopped the super zombie on its head. Its undead noggin whiplashed to the side. The super zombie straightened up and gave Ozzie a cackling chuckle. The blow hadn't even stunned it. The undead super freak rubbed the bump on its head and then charged at Ozzie again.

"Zack, get this crazy lady offa me!" Zoe shrieked as the super zombie rose from the deck of the ship and choked her with one hand and grabbed a handful of her hair with the other.

Zack raised the bat over his head and brought it down hard, but the super zombie woman's head shifted to one side, and the bat struck its shoulder instead. The undead super lady craned its neck halfway around to look at Zack. A horrible ripping noise sounded out like quickly pulled Velcro. Zack heard his sister let out a high-pitched screech.

"My hair!" Zoe shrieked. The super zombie had

pulled away a chunk of her brunette locks. "That does it!" Zoe rose to her feet. "Now you're going to get it, lady." She put up her fists like a trained prizefighter. "Nobody messes with my hair!"

The super zombie woman cackled.

Zoe unleashed a furious barrage of kicks and punches that landed square in the undead freak's face. The super zombie woman couldn't do anything as Zoe kept blasting it in the mouth.

WHAP! POW! WHAM! Zoe finished with a stiff uppercut that caught the super zombie woman under the chin and sent the zombie flipping over the side of the boat. The ravenous beast of a woman was unconscious before it even hit the water.

"Nice work, Zo," Zack said, and they bumped fists.

Behind them, Ozzie was still fending off his flaky, musclebound super zombie while Madison and Rice stood between the tall super zombie man and Olivia. The super zombie tried to plow through Rice and Madison. Madison slid the shaft of her golf club between its legs while Rice charged, bashing the uber undead mutant in

the gut with his elbow.
The super zombie
tripped and fell
with a splat on the
wooden deck.

"He's going
for Olivia!" Rice
shouted. "Olivia,
get belowdeck!"

Olivia turned and hurried quickly
down to the cabin.

Zack squinted toward the harbor to try to see what
was going on with the cruise ship. The motorized vessel
had crashed into the docks at the port and was now leaning to one side, crushing a couple yachts in the harbor.
The cruise ship wasn't going anywhere, but the rest of
the super zombies were abandoning the megaship and
swimming out to where the kids were.

"You guys," Zack shouted, "we gotta get out of here!
There are more super zombies coming!"

Ozzie jumped in the air, did a twisting sidespin,

and brought his leg down fast and hard against the muscled zombie. *BAM!* Ozzie's foot drilled the super zombie right in the temple. The undead freak stumbled back and fell over the stern of the ship.

"Where's the third one?" Zack asked, swiveling his head around the deck, baseball bat at the ready.

"We knocked him out already, dude," Rice said.

"You mean I knocked him out," Madison said proudly.

"Well, what'd you do with him?"

"He's right over th—" Rice started to say when Olivia's squeal rang out from down below. They all spun around as the door leading belowdeck was flung open. The tall super zombie man had Olivia slung over its shoulder.

"Hold it right there, you big weirdo!" Zoe shouted at the tall, lanky undead dude. "Put her down. Now!"

"Yeah, she's my cousin!" Madison yelled. "And if you mess with my family, you're messin' with me!"

The super zombie growled at the kids as Olivia kicked and screamed over its shoulder. "You want to do this the hard way, man?" Ozzie asked, and flipped his

homemade nunchaku under his arms and around his back. "We can do this the hard way. . . ." Ozzie lunged forward to bash the zombie's head in with the martial arts weapon, but before he had a chance, the super zombie heaved Olivia overboard.

KERPLUNK! Olivia dropped into the Caribbean.

BAM! BAM! BAM! Ozzie finished off the super zombie brute with a hard-striking nunchaku flurry.

The super zombie fell against the railing of the boat like a beat-up boxer leaning against the ropes. Ozzie

stepped forward. With a simple high kick, the undead lunatic vanished over the side and dropped into the ocean.

"Help!" Olivia screamed. "He's coming! He's coming!" She thrashed around in the water.

"Who's coming?" Zack shouted down to her.

"Ben!" she cried.

A buzz-saw sound grew closer and closer. Zack gasped as Cousin Ben zipped out of the morning mist, riding toward his sister on a Jet Ski.

Zack snatched up a length of rope from the ship and

threw it over the side. "Take that!" he called to her. She started to swim, doing the sidestroke to grab on to the end of the line.

"Hurry up!" Rice yelled. "Cousin Ben's closing in fast!"

Just as Olivia caught hold of the rope, Cousin Ben rode by with a whoosh and scooped her up out of the water.

Zack held tight to his end of the rope. "Don't worry, Olivia," he shouted to her, "I got you!"

As the Jet Ski zoomed off, Zack felt his feet leave the deck and he flew overboard, still hanging on to the rope as if the fate of the world depended on it.

Which it did.

CHAPTER 13

"Ahhh!" Zack shouted as the Jet Ski pulled him headfirst into the waves. Cousin Ben steered herky-jerky, zigzagging back and forth, trying to shake Zack off, but Zack held on to the rope with both hands.

"Let me go!" Olivia shrieked. Her brother had her firmly under his super strong arm. She tried to squirm free, but Cousin Ben's ironclad grip was far too powerful. Olivia gave up trying to get away and focused instead on holding on to the rope.

The super zombie Jet Ski weaved through the masses of zombie sea life. "Yow!" Zack yelped as something below the surface sank its teeth into his calf. A searing pain shot up his leg.

Zack was losing his grip. He couldn't keep this up much longer. But he couldn't let go. He desperately tried to tighten his grasp on the rope, the only thing connecting him to the last known zombie antidote.

The Jet Ski continued to cruise faster and faster, dragging him along. Cousin Ben turned his head back and saw Olivia clutching the rope and Zack still hydroplaning behind them on his stomach. The super zombie grunted and let out a dreadful top-of-the-food-chain roar that Zack could hear even over the revving motor.

Olivia shrieked as Cousin Ben hit a choppy wave and went airborne. They splashed down hard and Olivia lost hold of the rope.

Zack slowed to a stop in the bobbing water.

The super zombie Jet Ski sped away.

"Noooo!" Zack cried in desperation. He noticed a rustling in the water to his left. He felt the wake of Nigel's boat ripple toward him. Ozzie was trying to cut off the Jet Ski before Cousin Ben got any farther away.

Rice aimed the harpoon tranquilizer gun.

"Rice, don't!" Madison screamed. "You might hit Olivia!"

"Don't worry," Rice said. "I got 'im."

The Jet Ski zoomed across their path and Rice fired.

The harpoon whizzed right by Cousin Ben's head and into the water, missing by just a few inches. "Don't got 'im," said Rice.

Ozzie nudged Rice out of the way and quickly reloaded the harpoon gun with another tranquilizer.

"Hurry up, dude," Rice said. "He's getting away!"

"Just a second . . ." Ozzie eyed the target. The Jet Ski was cruising out of range fast. "Now!" Ozzie pulled the trigger.

WHAM! The tranquilizer tagged Cousin Ben in the upper thigh. The rope line on the harpoon tightened and yanked Cousin Ben violently off the watercraft. The Jet Ski corkscrewed in the air and came crashing down on its side. Cousin Ben and Olivia both belly flopped into the ocean.

Zack treaded water, looking around for Olivia. "Olivia!" he shouted. "Olivia!"

To his right, Zack could see a pack of zombie barracuda closing in on him. And the super zombies from the wrecked cruise ship were swimming toward him like they were in an ironman contest.

"Olivia!" Zack shouted. He was about to dive down when her head popped to the surface. She gasped for air and made a gargling sound before sinking back down. As Zack swam frantically toward her, she bobbed to the surface. She gurgled a mouthful of seawater and then spat out a lungful of fluid.

"Olivia!" Zack shouted. "You're okay!"

She coughed and hacked, then smiled at Zack as he helped to keep them both above water.

"Yeah," she said. "I'll be all right."

A few seconds later, Ozzie coasted Nigel's boat over and circled to a stop.

"Hold on," Rice said, grabbing a donut-shaped life preserver from the cabin. He swung it over his head like a cowboy about to fling a lasso and with a flick of his wrist launched it toward Zack and Olivia. Zoe threw a rope ladder over the side of the boat, and they climbed up before the barracuda or the super zombie swimmers could reach them.

"You guys okay?" Madison asked.

"I think so," Olivia said, still coughing a little.

Zack looked down at his leg. There was a large gash from whatever had bitten him. It was pretty nasty, but it wasn't the worst bite he'd ever received. At least he knew he wasn't going to zombify. He'd

been immune since the first outbreak.

"Where's Ben?" Olivia asked.

Cousin Ben floated facedown in the water, dangling from the harpoon line.

"We have to bring him back to Nigel's with us," Rice said.

"No way!" Zoe said. "That dude is not coming on our boat."

"We need him, Zoe," Rice said. "He's our only super zombie specimen right now."

"He's my brother, too, eh?" Olivia said. "Haul him up already."

Ozzie reeled him in, unhooked the tranquilizer harpoon from Cousin Ben's thigh, and laid him on the deck. His skin was pruned and puckered like a person's fingertips after bathing for too long.

"Come on," Ozzie said, revving the motor. "Let's get the heck out of here." Zack, Rice, and the girls zombie-proofed Cousin Ben by tying his arms and legs tightly with a reel of fishing wire.

With the giant frilled tiger shark and new super zombie specimen in tow, they cruised off into the bright Caribbean morning. They wanted to get back to Nigel's private island as quickly as they could.

Zack crossed his fingers tightly, hoping that Nigel Black was still safe where they'd left him.

CHAPTER 14

"Are we there yet?" Rice asked in a whiny voice.

Zoe peered over her sunglasses and shot him an evil glare. "Rice, you'd better not start that again."

"Relax, Zoe," said Rice. "I was just kidding. But seriously, are we there yet?"

"How much farther, Oz?" Zack shouted over to Ozzie.

"Not long," Ozzie responded.

"How long is not long?" Rice asked.

"Geez," Olivia said. "How old are you?"

Ahead of their boat, a creepy-looking fogbank hung

low on the water. As they passed through the fog, the outline of Nigel's private island emerged. It was about a day and a half later, and they were cruising through the Bahamas once again.

Zack felt his nerves start to jitter. When they approached the shoreline, he could see the burned-out super zombie's pirate ship beached in the sand. The air was still and quiet as Zack looked through the binoculars and scanned the exterior of Nigel's zombie-proof fortress. There wasn't a super zombie in view. But that didn't mean they weren't hiding.

"Ozzie!" Zack called to his friend. "Take her around back."

"You got it!" Ozzie shouted back. He navigated the boat into the narrow beach cove that led into Nigel's underground doomsday bunker.

Zack hopped down and saw the shuffled footprints of super zombies stamped in the sandy turf.

He sprinted through the dark cave to the entrance of the bunker. Super zombie pummel marks dented the steel door. Zack pounded the door with both fists. "Nigel! Nigel, open up, it's us!"

There was no answer.

Zack walked back to the boat, hanging his head for another fallen friend. He looked up at the rest of the group. "I don't think he's here!" Zack said to them, sounding a little panicked.

"Do you think the super zombies got him?" Olivia asked.

"I don't know," Zack said. "Maybe?"

Twinkles ran up to Zack's feet and whined at him.

"I can't believe we did all this for nothing."

"Now what kind of zombie expert would I be if I let a few super zombies get the best of me?" Nigel Black's voice echoed through the cavern.

Zack spun around on his heel. He let out a deep sigh of relief at the sight of the former sea explorer and present zombie expert.

The kids all jumped off the boat and ran up to Nigel. "We thought the super zombies got you!" Madison said.

"It was close," Nigel said. "But once I activated the electric fence and zapped a few of them, they just took off on the cruise ship."

"Are you sure they're all gone?" Zack asked.

"Yes, I'm sure. Now, how did you fare on your expedition?" he asked them.

"We did it," Zack told him. "We caught the giant frilled tiger shark down in Jamaica, and we have a super zombie to test the new antidote on."

Nigel's eyes lit up as he rushed past them toward the boat. He looked inside the compartment beneath the boat. His eyes became misty at the sight of the frilled shark. "I must say, I'm very impressed," he said. "You've

done what I thought no one could do. Now we must act quickly and transport this animal into my lab for testing."

Everyone sprang into action. Nigel rushed back into the subterranean section of his island bunker. The kids dragged Cousin Ben, who was still tranquilized, off the boat. Nigel returned, lugging what looked like a large stretcher behind him.

"Here," he said, laying the stretcher on the ground by the boat. They unloaded the giant frilled tiger shark off the boat and onto the stretcher, then hauled the great beast inside. The girls followed with Cousin Ben in tow.

Nigel's laboratory was state of the art with all kinds of medical equipment and supplies.

"Strap him down," Nigel told them. "We don't want him waking up on us, do we?"

Madison and Olivia plopped Ben on an examination table and buckled his arms and legs into the restraints.

On the other side of the lab, Zack, Rice, and Ozzie struggled to hoist the giant frilled tiger shark into an aquarium tank. "Ugh!" Rice said. "This thing weighs a ton!"

Nigel walked over to the tank and inspected the incapacitated giant frilled tiger shark. "Time to run a few tests."

They all watched while Nigel stepped up to the enormous fish. "Scalpel," he said, and put his hand out. Rice handed their zombie expert a knife. Nigel made an incision across the giant frilled tiger shark's abdomen.

"So nasty." Madison and Olivia jinxed each other, closing their eyes tightly.

"Syringe," Nigel said, handing Rice the scalpel
back. Nigel then peeled back the frilled shark's skin
and pierced the sea monster's stomach with the needle.
Zack cringed at the sight of the massive fish's innards.
Nigel carefully extracted the massive shark's digestive
enzymes, then sewed the large sea beast back together.

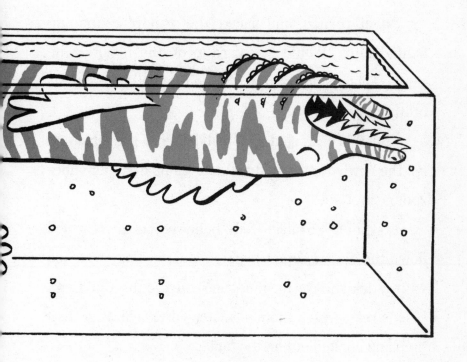

"Gumball," he said to Rice.

Rice reached into his bag and pulled out one of the few remaining antidote gumballs. Nigel injected the new ingredient into the hard candy. Carrying the freshly injected gumball, he walked over to Cousin Ben, strapped to the gurney.

Cousin Ben's super zombie eyes popped open from his tranquil slumber. He began writhing on the table but couldn't break free of the restraints.

Nigel turned and faced the children standing behind him. "Would you care to do the honors?" he said to Olivia, and handed her the gumball. "He is your brother after all."

"Sure," Olivia said. She walked up to the table and fed the newly formulated antidote gumball to her super zombie brother.

"Braiiins!" Cousin Ben bellowed as he gargled down the chewy super zombie antidote. They watched with anticipation as the medicine coursed through Ben's bloodstream. A few moments later, Olivia's brother went limp and conked out on the table.

"Is it working?" Zack asked.

"Be patient," Nigel said, observing his test subject with great interest.

Cousin Ben jerked awake with startling swiftness. His eyes shot open again. The hateful super zombie gleam was gone from his gaze. "Where am I?"

he asked in a normal human voice.

"Ben!" Olivia rushed over to her brother's side. "You're okay!"

A befuddled scowl crossed his face. "Olivia?" he asked. "What's going on?" He paused. "I don't . . . I don't feel so good."

Right before their eyes, Ben's features contorted. He grimaced in brain-crazed agony as the super zombie virus fought against the new serum. Still bound by the restraints, his spine arched to a backbreaking degree. With a subhuman scream of pure pain and rage, he slumped back down.

"What's going on?" Olivia asked Nigel. Terror shone in her eyes.

Cousin Ben's eyes reopened. The super zombie glare was back once again. Nigel rushed to the side of the table. Cousin Ben yapped at the zombie expert and bit at the air, grunting and growling.

Nigel scratched his head. "I don't know. The shark enzyme by itself must not have been enough to override the jellyfish DNA in this virus strain."

"Come on, man," Zoe said. "We went all that way for nothing?"

"Not for nothing," Nigel said. "The shark enzyme did do something, but it just didn't fix him completely."

"Well, that's kind of the whole point, dude," Rice said. "What do we do now?"

"Don't lose hope. I still think we're on the right track." Nigel took out a large needle and extracted a blood sample from Cousin Ben's leg. "I'll run some more

tests and see if I can figure out what went wrong."

"Do you need any help?" Zack asked.

"No, I'll be okay," he said. "Just keep an eye on your super zombie friend. I'll be back shortly."

Nigel disappeared into the back of the laboratory, and the kids looked at one another in disbelief.

"Did you see him?" Olivia said. "It was like he was

two completely different people."

"Do you think Nigel will be able to fix the serum?" Rice asked.

"Don't know, Rice," said Zack. "I hope so."

A short while later, Nigel came out of the lab and approached Zack and the gang. "It looks like we're going to need a few other things to complete the serum. The frilled shark's digestive enzyme is doing its job, but it isn't enough to reverse the super zombie virus on its own. We're also going to need a specific chemical compound that will shorten the life span of the virus."

"Well, where can we get that?" Zack asked.

"The particular compound we need can be found only in the African mayfly, known to be abundant on the riverbanks of Madagascar. Since the mayfly has the shortest known life span of any creature on Earth, its chemical makeup will shorten the duration of the super zombie virus. You'll have to travel to Madagascar and gather up the unhatched larvae from the riverbanks of the jungle. I'll keep Ben sedated here with me until you return."

"Well, you guys," Zack said, turning to his friends. "Looks like we've got a little traveling to do."

"Ugh," said Zoe. "I'm so not packed for Madagascar. . . ."

"Yeah," said Madison. "We're totally gonna need to do some shopping before we go."

Zack looked at Rice and Ozzie, and the boys all shook their heads.

Some things never change, he thought, and smiled inwardly. *Even in a world full of zombies trying to eat your brains.*

The smile quickly faded from Zack's face. Sure, they had wrangled the main ingredient for the super zombie antidote and managed to capture a super zombie specimen. But they still had a long way to go to save the world again. The undead war was far from over.

But what else was new?

Where in the undead world
will the Zombie Chasers go next?
Find out in:

CHEWS
YOUR OWN
ADVENTURE

ALIEN INVASION!
READ ON FOR A LOOK AT JOHN KLOEPFER'S
OUT-OF-THIS-WORLD SERIES

The satellite dish tilted upward, aiming itself at the night sky. Kevin gave the thumbs-up and TJ hit the send button. Kevin felt his stomach clench as the laser refracted through the prism, shot out through the satellite dish, and carried their message to the universe across the black, starry night.

"So what happens now?" Kevin asked.

"We wait for the aliens," said Warner. "Obviously."

Kevin settled cross-legged into the grass and started to jot down the sequence of events in his log.

11:30 p.m.: No response yet.
11:37 p.m.: Tara challenges Warner and TJ to a staring contest. Warner blinks first. TJ wins.
11:38 p.m.: Warner challenges Tara to a laughing contest because that's what he thought they were doing in the first place. Tara laughs first.
11:45 p.m.: My butt is getting wet from the wet grass. Should have brought a towel.
11:50 p.m.: Everybody cranky. Warner regrets not bringing snacks. We all regret the no snack bringing, too.
12:00 a.m.: Galactascope still silent.

As Kevin marked the mission failure into his log, he felt his stomach tighten with panic. Even if there were aliens out there, it could take months for them to get the message, and they only had a few days before the convention.

"Come on, guys," Kevin said, his face crestfallen. "Let's pack up and get out of here before we get in trouble. We can try again tomorrow."

"Are you sure you don't want to wait a little longer, Kev?" Tara asked. "I could stay up a little laaaaaay-ter." She yawned, stretching her arms out.

THUNK! Tara's wrist whacked the device, and the galactascope abruptly began to blip and bleep. The laptop monitor flashed to life, and a long, repetitive jumble of ones and zeroes appeared on the screen.

"What'd you do?" Warner asked.

"I didn't mean to!" Tara scowled at Warner then looked at the computer. "What the heck is that?"

"It's a message," Kevin whispered, his voice tinged with anticipation.

They watched as the coded message scrolled down the computer screen, stopping abruptly and morphing into English through a neat little translator programming code that TJ had installed. "SOS. Need interstellar coordinates. SOS. Need interstellar coordinates. SOS."

"Quick," Warner said. "Send it a map of our solar system."

TJ typed frantically on the laptop, pulling up a diagram of Earth's solar system.

"Now give it our longitude and latitude," said Kevin.

They waited in suspense by the lakeside, hoping for a reply. "I don't know," Kevin said, beginning to get discouraged after ten minutes of silence. "Maybe someone's messing with us?"

"But no one knows we're even out here," Warner said.

Alexander, Kevin thought. *Is he spying on us?*

"Come on, Kevin," said Tara. "It has to be real. Let's try it again." She turned to TJ. "Resend the coordinates, Teej."

TJ nodded, interlocking his fingers and pushing out the palms of his hands. As his knuckles cracked, the night sky suddenly opened up with a bright neon-blue flash.

"Whoa," Warner and Tara said together.

Kevin blinked twice, completely speechless. He squinted and watched as a speck of otherworldly light started to grow against the dark backdrop of the sky. At first it looked like a normal star, but as the speck became larger and larger, Kevin could see a UFO hurtling toward them on a billowing trail of gray smoke. *This can't really be happening.*

"Get down!" Kevin shouted as the UFO flew right over their heads.

The four of them ducked for cover as the spacecraft crashed into the lake, sending a large wave rippling toward the shore.

"Holy Moley Mother of Cannoli!" TJ spoke for the first time since the beginning of camp. "Did you just see that?"

Tara, Warner, and Kevin all turned their heads to TJ.

"Dude," Warner said. "I totally forgot you even knew how to talk."

Kevin swiveled his head back and forth, waiting for one of their counselors to check out the commotion, but the camp was still.

"Omigosh," Tara cried out, pointing toward the center of the lake. Something had burst to the surface and was flailing frantically in the water.

"It can't swim," Kevin shouted, and ran toward the paddleboats that were beached on the lakeshore. "We gotta save it! Come on!"

ACKNOWLEDGMENTS

Many sincere thanks to Emilia Rhodes for helping me navigate through the rough, zombie-infested waters; to Josh Bank and Sara Shandler for throwing me some bait; to Alice Jerman and Sarah Landis for reeling me in and not letting me drift; and to Ryan Harbage for helping me catch the big fish.

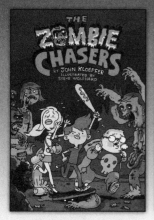
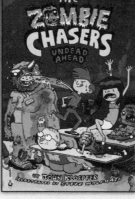

New from
JOHN KLOEPFER,
the author of
THE ZOMBIE CHASERS

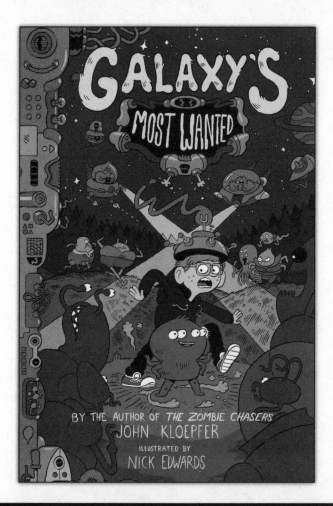